W9-CEV-754

**To my brothers,
Doug, Mike, and Tim.
Mike loved space.
He's watching us from there.**

MARGARET K. McELDERRY BOOKS
An imprint of Simon & Schuster Children's Publishing Division
1230 Avenue of the Americas, New York, New York 10020
Text copyright © 2015 by Kevin Sylvester
Illustrations copyright © 2015 by Dominic Harmon
MARGARET K. McELDERRY BOOKS is a trademark of Simon & Schuster, Inc.
For information about special discounts for bulk purchases, please contact Simon & Schuster Special Sales at 1-866-506-1949 or business@simonandschuster.com.
The Simon & Schuster Speakers Bureau can bring authors to your live event. For more information or to book an event, contact the Simon & Schuster Speakers Bureau at 1-866-248-3049 or visit our website at www.simonspeakers.com.
Book design by Sonia Chaghatzbanian
The text for this book is set in ITC Garamond Std.
Manufactured in the United States of America
0815 FFG
10 9 8 7 6 5 4 3 2 1
Library of Congress Cataloging-in-Publication Data
Sylvester, Kevin.
Miners / Kevin Sylvester. — First edition.
pages cm
Summary: "Twelve-year-old Christopher Nichols and his family live on a new planet, Perses, as colonists of Melming Mining's Great Mission to save the Earth. When Landers, as the attackers are called, obliterate the colony to steal the metal and raw ore, Christopher and a small group of survivors are forced into the maze of mining tunnels below the surface of Perses"— Provided by publisher.
ISBN 978-1-4814-4039-4 (hardcover)
ISBN 978-1-4814-4041-7 (eBook)
[1. Space colonies—Fiction. 2. Mines and mineral resources—Fiction. 3. Survival—Fiction. 4. Science fiction.] I. Title.
PZ7.S98348Mi 2015
[Fic]—dc23   2014049696

FIRST
EDITION

MINRS

KEVIN SYLVESTER

MARGARET K. McELDERRY BOOKS
New York London Toronto Sydney New Delhi

Chapter One

CALCULATIONS

The Earth blinked, and was gone.

I squinted through my binoculars just to be sure. My elbows dug into the dust and pebbles as I steadied my arms on the ground.

Nothing but thousands and thousands of stars stared back at me.

Earth had definitely dipped below the horizon, a full five minutes earlier than the night before. My calculations were right. This also meant I'd found the perfect spot for a big Blackout party.

I got up and brushed off my pants. I paused for a moment to take in the night sky and the flat rocky landscape.

It was cool having no moon. You could see every star so clearly. It was quiet, beautiful, peaceful.

The starlight reflected off the collection pools nearby, reminding me of fireflies back on Earth. I wondered if the adults would actually let us go swimming in one of the pools, just for Blackout night. If the littler kids promised not to pee in them, maybe? No, fat chance of that happening. We filtered the water before we drank it, but the adults still worried about stuff all the time. Adults are always worrying about something.

The temperature began to drop, and the wind picked up, sending tiny waves across the surface of the pools, making the fireflies dance. I turned around and headed back to the compound, running through my calculations one more time.

Five minutes a day. That meant the Blackout was going to arrive in the next week and a half.

My parents had been telling me this, and the constant news reports had too, but I wanted to work it out for myself. If I had to predict, and I didn't have to but wanted to, the Blackout would begin at 6:11:23 p.m. the following Saturday.

Of course, no one was sure what would happen next.

I couldn't wait to tell my dad I was right. And I knew

exactly where to find him: just ending his shift in the mines.

I stepped onto the roof of the core-scraper. "Elevator, please," I said.

A hole opened in the roof, and a grimy metal box rose up. Two *M*s had been etched onto the doors, the logo for the Melming Mining Corporation. The *M*s split apart as the elevator opened and a voice said, *"Please watch your step."*

The elevator had a woman's voice, but it was a little tinny, like a computer from the old movies we sometimes watched in class. My dad told me the original voice sounded too human, and it made everyone nervous. So the programmers recalibrated the voices on all the equipment to be just slightly off, even though they could have made them perfect.

It bugged me every time I heard one. Melming Mining had done so many things right, like sending us into space to live, so why accept second best when you didn't have to?

I stepped inside.

"Seventy-fifth floor, please," I said, and the doors closed.

As the elevator began to descend, the video screen blipped to life. Messages flashed across the screen.

The Great Mission Is Everyone's Mission.

You are what makes it great.

Melming Mining is a green company.

Remember to always compost your waste.

Put people ahead of profit.

Safety first.

Perses is our home.

We are all caretakers.

Earth thanks you for your sacrifice and your bravery.

The messages were all over the place, on posters in our classroom, the walls of our core-scraper, and the tunnels of the mines.

Each time I saw one, I felt my chest swell with pride. Melming Mining wasn't just an employer. The company had helped save Earth. It had helped colonize Perses, the planetoid the elevator was now dropping deep inside.

Hans Melming, the man behind the company, was a genius and a scientist of almost unlimited creativity. He was one of my heroes.

And I was part of his Great Mission.

"We have arrived at the seventy-fifth floor," said the tinny woman.

The doors slid open, and musty cool air rushed into the elevator. I smiled. The mines were my favorite place to explore, even more than the surface. My best friend, Elena, and I sometimes snuck down here to look around. Elena's dad was a foreman, and she knew all the best places, like the break room off Tunnel 2 that had a door that didn't lock and a stash of chocolate bars and potato chips for the taking.

I stepped out into a gigantic hall carved from solid rock. The jagged teeth of an enormous blast door hovered above me. I knew the door was there to protect us in case the miners accidentally set off anything explosive, like a pocket of gas or some unstable ore, but it still looked like the fangs of a giant monster. I had to force myself to pass underneath.

A huge opening at the far end of the hall led to the actual tunnels. There were four main tunnels, with dozens and dozens of subtunnels branching off from them. My dad said it was a like a giant maze the farther and farther you got from the entrance.

Doorways dotted the left-hand side of the hall, leading to the bathrooms and an infirmary. Once, I'd tripped and cut my head during a not-so-authorized visit and had been stitched up there by Dr. Singh.

Mom had not been happy. Dad thought it was kind of amusing, but still backed up her decision to ground me for the weekend.

Rows of lockers spread out along the right wall. Some contained equipment, blasting caps, shovels, and fire extinguishers, while the others were lockers for the workers. Miners were coming back from inside the tunnels, taking off their helmets, boots, and orange jumpsuits.

The Sunlites above were beginning to fade, mimicking the fading light of a sunset, and pink and gold began to tinge the smooth walls. It was a clever and nice way to signal the end of the workday. I grinned. Melming thought of everything.

I looked for my father and saw him at the far end of the hall, unstrapping his helmet and talking with one of the other miners. They were laughing. My father was a manager, but had been a miner when he was younger. He seemed to get along with everybody.

"Dad!" I called.

"Well, it's my son, the genius!" He beamed as I ran up to him. He slapped me on the shoulder as I held up my notebook.

"Look, my calculations were right!"

My dad took the notebook in his huge hands and examined the numbers, nodding thoughtfully as he turned the pages. "Nice work. It's good to know there's someone keeping those scientists and bigwigs on the third floor honest."

The miner next to him, I think it was Mr. Spirin, but it was hard to tell with the rock dust on his face, laughed.

Dad was always saying stuff like that—suggesting someone in the upper floors was doing something a little sneaky. He and my mom would argue over that when he got really cynical. She was a teacher (*my* teacher here on Perses, ugh), but was also from a mining family, and would say, "Jim, please don't," or, "Christopher doesn't need to hear that," or even, "If it's so bad, then why don't we catch the next shuttle home?" But she was always smiling when they got into these arguments, and he was too.

I knew he was kidding. My dad even had a Melming Mining tattoo on his arm. His work clothes usually covered it, but I'd caught a glimpse of the double *M*s once or twice when he was walking around the apartment in short sleeves. That tattoo was proof he believed in this mission as much as anyone.

He handed me back the notebook. "Well, there's no denying the Blackout is coming, and on schedule," he said. He was smiling, but his voice sounded quiet, like he was distracted.

An alarm rang from the tunnels. Another miner ran up to my father, hands waving. "There's been a cave-in in the new section of Tunnel Four."

"Big?"

The miner shook his head. "No, but the digger hit an air pocket, and some loose rock fell."

"Anyone trapped?" my father asked, strapping on his helmet.

The man shook his head. "The digger cone got smashed. We can't account for two grinders, but no miners got trapped, thank goodness."

My dad's face twisted in a grimace as he turned to me. "I've got to check this out. You head back home."

"Can't I come with you?" I asked.

Dad shook his head. "Too dangerous. Tell your mother I'll be up in a bit." Then he turned and marched away, the limp from his injured leg barely slowing him down.

I watched him disappear, then walked to the elevator, lost in thought. Too dangerous? My dad had let me inside the tunnels. Sure, there'd never been a cave-in before, but how dangerous could they be, really? *No miners were trapped.* I'd heard that with my own ears.

The doors slid open as soon as I reached the elevator,

and I smacked right into Elena, who was coming out.

"Ouch!" we said at the same time, grabbing our noses and mouths.

"Watch where you're going!" she said, leaning back against the metal door and checking to make sure she wasn't bleeding.

"Sorry, I was thinking."

"That's a shock," she said.

Elena bent down to pick up a tin thermos she'd dropped, and I bent down to pick up my notebook.

Of course, we did this at the same time as well, knocking our foreheads together with an audible thud.

Elena stood up and rubbed her head. "Hey, Einstein! I'll go first. You get your head back here on Perses."

I nodded, feeling a little dizzy. After Elena stood back up, I reached down and grabbed the notebook.

She pointed at the numbers and notes on the open page. "Those about the Blackout?"

"Yeah. I know exactly when it's going to happen, and there will still be lots of daylight. I think it will help convince our parents to let us have the party."

She pumped her fist in the air. "Yes!" Elena was always complaining about how boring things could get on Perses. The idea of a big party had become almost an obsession.

"I think we can even start making some plans."

Elena beamed at me. "Nice work, Christopher!"

I loved it when Elena smiled at me. Elena and her family had flown next to us on the shuttle from Earth six years before, and she'd practically forced me to share the cookies I'd brought with me. We'd been best friends ever since.

"Hey, I've got a couple of minutes. We could do some planning now," I said.

She held up the thermos. "Can't. I'm here to bring dinner to my dad. He's working a later shift tonight or something. I'm supposed to go look for him. Wanna come?"

I knew from experience that "looking" for anything with Elena would end up with us lost and combing through dark places for hours. The last thing I needed to do was get my parents mad at me for exploring the tunnels without permission, especially when I needed their support for the party.

"Actually, I should get back up for dinner," I said.

Elena frowned, but not for long.

"Oh!" she added. "I forgot to tell you. I just got an awesome new book on the Napoleonic Wars from the library. I think I can even tie it in to that stupid assignment your mom gave us on food history. Sorry, I mean that really, *really* important assignment."

"Very funny," I said, mocking a laugh. "I bet it's a natural fit. Didn't they invent canned food for one of those wars?"

Elena winked. "Great minds think alike. Anyway, the file is from a library on Earth, so I need to read it before the Blackout."

"Got it. Enjoy." Military history was definitely not my thing, even if Elena made it sound thrilling.

"But I can get together tomorrow," she said.

"Okay. That would be cool."

"Great. Let's meet before school starts."

I gave a thumbs-up.

She turned and began to walk away.

I called out, suddenly hoping she'd stay and chat some more. "I've got some other stuff about the Blackout I can show you if we meet up top."

She turned and rolled her eyes. "Knowing you, it's probably math. But cool. Gotta go. Before school, at the field." She pointed to the surface.

"Perfect. Great," I said.

Elena turned, giving me a little wave. I watched her until the doors slid closed. Then I just stood there, thinking about her, and how her enthusiasm for stuff was so contagious.

"Floor number, please," said the electronic woman.

"Fifteenth floor," I said, and the elevator began to rise.

More slogans ran across the screen.

I didn't read them this time. I was too busy coming up with a plan to make Elena's party really happen.

Chapter Two
Plans

The next morning I woke up early, slid on a clean pair of jeans and a button-down shirt, and grabbed my backpack. I stopped in front of the bathroom mirror and made sure my shirt was on properly and then ran a comb through my hair, trying as best I could to get the tight curls to behave. I took a deep breath and practiced my smile.

Elena would be waiting for me up top, but I had to do something down here first—get Mom and Dad on side with the idea of a Blackout party. A teacher and a manager would hold a lot of sway. Elena and I had come up with the idea, but it was no use planning specifics if the adults were just going to kill it straight off.

Mom was in the kitchen, packing up lunches. Dad was sitting at the table, reading some report and finishing off a plate of eggs and fried potatoes.

The eggs smelled slightly chalky, like they'd been made from one of the pre-mixes we'd brought with us from Earth. But the home fries smelled amazing. I smiled.

"Are those potatoes from here?" I asked eagerly, making my smile even bigger.

Dad nodded. "Yup. The first crop from the new agri-zone. The terra-forming is really working well. It was all just rock a few months ago. Amazing." He slid the plate over to me, and I eagerly gulped down a forkful.

"These *are* amazing!" I beamed. Then I turned on the charm. "Mom. You are a genius with home fries! A genius!"

Mom stepped into the room, hands on her hips.

"What are you after?" she said, narrowing her eyes.

My smile faded.

Dad let out a huge belly laugh.

"Don't try the sweet talk, son. Your mother has special radar. Melming has been trying to steal her secret for years."

She walked over and gave him a good-natured swat on the shoulder.

"And that's why it's stayed a secret!" he said. "Not worth the risk."

She laughed and swatted him again.

"Okay, you win," I said, trying to wrap this up quickly. "I am after something."

"So why the sweet talk *and* the clean shirt? It must be *huge*," Mom said, turning her attention back to me.

I took a deep breath. "It might be."

"Honesty is always the best policy," Mom said, taking a seat at the table and popping a home fry into her mouth. "Although you are right—I am a genius with these things. So, what are you after?"

"Okay, you know how everyone is worried about the Blackout."

Mom and Dad exchanged glances. There were traces of frowns on their lips, or was I imagining that? "I don't know if *worried* is the right word," Mom said.

"It's just that it's something new," Dad said. "We've never gone through one before."

"I know. It's just that—" I started, but they kept going on without me.

"It's a stupid name," Mom said. "The Sun isn't going anywhere. We're not going to be in total darkness or anything. No wonder the kids are worried."

"I'm not—" I started, but they ignored me.

"It is a communications blackout. I didn't pick the name," Dad said.

Mom went on. "Why not call it the Perses Break or Vacation? That's all it is, a break from the Earth for a while." She looked at me and turned on her teacher voice. "The Earth and Perses will only be on opposite sides of the Sun for a short time."

"Too much noise from the radiation. Can't talk," Dad said.

Mom nodded. "It's more like we're going on an unplugged vacation for the summer. No computer chats, no texting, no phone calls, no contact. But life continues on as normal here on Perses and on Earth."

"Then in two months we'll get back together for a big 'family reunion' and compare notes."

"Nothing to worry about," they finished together.

"I'm *not* worried," I said a little too loudly. I needed to get this conversation back on track. "I think it's cool, actually. But I know that lots of kids are just kind of freaked out a bit. Some of the adults, too, and don't deny it."

My parents stole looks at each other again.

"I'm just wondering if, rather than talking about it like a big mysterious thing all the time, we could celebrate the Blackout. Maybe we could do something fun to show how cool it is that we're in space and that this thing is happening here."

"You mean, like throw a party?" my Mom said.

"That's an *awesome* idea," I said, beaming. "Wow! A party would be great!"

"Hmmmmm," my dad said, rubbing his chin with his fingers. "It might be just the thing to get everyone relaxed."

"We could even invite all the farmers to come over for the day, have some games for the kids," Mom said.

Dad nodded. "We don't all get together enough."

A rush of excitement ran through me. "The Sun will still be up when Earth disappears. Elena and I have already made some plans for snacks—chips and chocolate cakes. And maybe we could shoot off fireworks."

Mom narrowed her eyes at me again, a smile playing on her lips. "So, a party is an awesome idea. I'm *soooo* glad I thought it up on my own."

"See, son," Dad said, tapping a finger against his head. "Special radar."

"But it *is* a good idea, right?" I hoped I hadn't blown it. Why didn't I know when to keep quiet?

Mom walked back into the kitchen. "We'll think about it. Now, get moving or you'll be late for school. There's an assembly today. First period. Mandatory."

I slid off my chair. "Okay, but promise me you'll think about it?"

Dad nodded and winked. Mom continued folding up the paper bags for lunch but said, "Promise."

I walked into the hallway. I thought I heard them both sigh, but it might have been the front door swishing closed behind me.

I hoped Elena was still waiting for me on the outdoor field. The field was the one grassy bit on our quadrant of Perses. It used up precious water and terra-firmed soil, but stepping onto the cushy grass in bare feet was like being instantly transported home, so everyone put in a little time and sacrificed a little water to keep it growing.

It was also where we had gym class, so we kids felt like we had first dibs.

There was a poster just outside the school office that proved it was meant for us.

MELMING ACADEMY BELIEVES IN FRESH AIR AND EXERCISE.
THEY HELP BUILD A HEALTHY AND HAPPY STUDENT BODY.

So I wasn't too surprised when the elevator doors opened, and there was a whole crowd of kids chatting with Elena.

My spirits fell—a little bit anyway. I'd been hoping it would just be us two.

Instead almost our entire class was there—Alek Lotar, Pavel Spirin, Brock Louis, Jimmi Murphy, Maria Agneli, and Mandeep Singh. Some of the little kids from the primary class were up top too, swinging and climbing on the field's playground.

We all came from different backgrounds and countries. Jimmi was actually the son of the general manager of the colony, the head honcho for the whole Perses operation. Most were from miner families. Some were the kids of the scientists or, in my case, managers. But we all got along pretty well. We had to. There were only about twenty kids total on Perses, and only half of those were as old as we were, so you couldn't really afford to be too much of a jerk.

Jimmi saw me first. "Hey, it's Little Melming!" he called out. "How's the superbrain today?"

I stopped, unsure if it was a compliment or a jab.

Elena frowned at him, clearly convinced it was the second. "Well, we all know *your* brain doesn't work, Little Murphy."

Everyone laughed, even Jimmi, although his face flushed red a bit as well.

Elena waved me over. "Okay, Fearless Leader, tell us what you've found out."

I sat down on the field and opened up my notebook.

"The Blackout is going to happen just before sunset, but we'll still have about a half hour of daylight left."

Mandeep gave a cheer. "So we can have a party where even the little kids can stay up."

Elena nodded. "The adults will like that."

"There's only a couple of *really* little kids," said Maria. Her sister, Angela, was born here and had just turned four. "I'll start working on my parents."

"Good idea," I said. "My parents bought in already. I think they'll pitch it to management."

Jimmi snorted. "Don't you think that would have more weight coming from *me*?" His tone annoyed me, but he had a point.

"I think that's a great idea, Jimmi," I said, smiling and hoping he didn't have the same radar as my mom. "So, let's move on to some details."

Pavel pointed to the center of the field. "We could put the tables around there in a kind of circle, and then do games where we go around the outside, like Perses around the Sun."

"Cool! Orbital musical chairs," Brock said. "I'll pick the music."

"I have a great idea for the music!" came a voice from behind me. Finn Shannon ran up. He'd only been promoted to our class this year. He must have seen us talking, and then came over. "Why don't we tune into a radio station on Earth? We can get them to play us some Blackout songs and maybe even send some messages!"

Everyone thought about this for a second. "Maybe they'll take requests," Maria said.

"And we can send some messages to our families back home."

"We'll all be listening together."

"Could be really cool," Elena said. "The Blackout Party officially ends when the music ends."

Jimmi looked skeptical. "Would that even work?"

Everyone turned toward me. Little Melming the science guy. "Actually, yes," I said. "There would be a delay because of the distance, and some of it would get distorted as we got closer to the actual Blackout, but for the most part we could make it work with a little coordination. It's a good idea, Finn."

Finn beamed.

Everyone threw out more ideas for foods, snacks, cakes, and even costumes, and I hurried to write them down in my notebook.

The school bell rang out from the core-scraper.

"Ugh, school." Alek groaned.

"At least we have an assembly to start things off," Maria said.

Jimmi shrugged. "My dad is giving some kind of rah-rah speech." He was trying to sound disinterested, but you could tell by how straight he was standing that he was proud.

"I hear we're watching the Great Mission movie again," said Alek. "I can recite that thing from memory."

"And my mom is going to go over emergency procedures all week," Mandeep said.

"Sounds great," Pavel said, but I didn't need special radar to know he was being sarcastic.

"*That* should help the little kids not get nervous!" Maria joked.

The bell rang again.

Everyone began walking toward the elevators. Elena reached out and tugged at my shoulder. "Can I talk to you for a sec?" she whispered.

"Um, sure," I said.

Elena kicked a stone as the other kids disappeared into the core-scraper's elevators. The gravity on Perses was slightly weaker than on Earth, and the stone flew, pinging off the metal support of the swing set.

"Nice shot," I said. "But I bet I can match it." I pulled back my foot and prepared to send a pebble zinging into the distance, but Elena didn't trash-talk me at all, which was odd, so I stopped.

Her eyebrows were furrowed. She was biting her bottom lip.

"Everything okay?" I asked.

"Yesterday, when I was looking for my dad, I went to one of the break rooms. I could hear everyone arguing inside, but as soon as I opened the door, they just stared at me with these fake smiles, and shut up. I'm not a little kid anymore. I can tell they're nervous about the Blackout."

"It seems pretty normal. We don't really know what's going to happen. The Sun could send out a flare at the wrong moment and fry all our tech. Although, at least that would shut up that voice on the elevators."

Elena chuckled. "And I guess the school bell won't work anymore."

"Or the terra-forming equipment," I said, then winced, realizing this wasn't actually that funny.

Elena's smile vanished. "I think my dad and mom wanted to go back to Earth to wait it out."

I flinched. Elena had almost gone back? The thought of life on Perses without her around was . . . horrible.

She kicked another stone and watched as it flew away.

The school bell rang a third time.

"We'd better get going," I said. The thought of my

mother's eyes boring into me as I walked into the assembly late made me shudder.

"They're just showing that dumb movie again," Elena said, but she began walking back to the core-scraper.

"That's my favorite movie!" I said, and I meant it. It was a history of the Great Mission and the near collision between Earth and Perses. I loved it.

Elena clearly didn't.

"Why did they even bring kids here?" she asked as the elevator doors slid open.

"I'm glad they did. This is an adventure."

"Uh-huh," she said, rolling her eyes. "Tenth floor," she said.

"You have two minutes until school begins," said the elevator.

"An adventure with elevators that think they're your mother," she said.

"Imagine the elevator is a ship."

Elena took in the walls of the shiny metal box. "I'll try."

"Back in the age of exploration, merchants and sailors—and lots of them were *our* age—they would head out on ships to who knows where. Maybe just some rumor of an interesting place."

"Here we go again," she said under her breath.

"They would be gone for months with no way to talk

to anyone back home. Some never came back—lost at sea, or shipwrecked on a deserted island, dead from disease—but more still went out each year. Why?"

"Because it was *exciting*," she said, doing her best to mimic my voice.

"Yes! More and more died, more and more explored. They made the modern world as we know it."

"They also did a lot of bad stuff, like stealing land, killing the people they found."

I waved my hands. "Sure, sure. I know. But we don't do that anymore. The main point is the adventure. And that hasn't changed. If you don't take risks, you'll never see what's possible."

Elena slumped as the elevator began to slow down, but I was warming into my speech.

"The ones who did come back returned with riches, gold, new foods, minerals, spices. That's what we're doing here. We're taking risks, but trying to save life back on Earth. And I'd rather be here than—"

"You have arrived at the tenth floor," interrupted the elevator.

We stepped out. The auditorium doors were closing, and we slipped in just in time. The auditorium was barely a third full, but Elena grabbed two seats in the last row. We settled in, and I continued my speech.

"I feel like a modern-day Magellan or James Cook, and that wouldn't happen on Earth anymore."

"You read too many adventure stories," Elena said.

"Those guys were amazing."

Elena shrugged. "Those guys were okay, but they weren't as cool as Caesar or Alexander the Great. Those guys kicked butt. And they wanted everyone to know it. They'd win these big battles and then build huge monuments to show everyone how much butt they'd kicked. They'd have huge parades with prisoners and elephants. Then they'd have huge feasts that would last for days."

"Are you suggesting we have some elephants at the Blackout Bash?"

"Ha-ha. No." Then she got very quiet. She turned to me, her brown eyes staring deep into mine. "Christopher. You're the smartest person I know. Is there really a reason to be nervous about the Blackout?"

She leaned in close and touched my hand. The truth was that I didn't know, or I did know but didn't want to say, things could go wrong. Something in her eyes told me she wanted assurance, and she wanted it from me.

"Nothing a good party can't solve," I said, smiling.

She nodded and smiled back, keeping her hand on mine. "Good. Then a party it is. And if everything goes all *pshfhgfhttttt*"—she made a kind of spitting noise—"at least we'll be part of history!"

"Maybe they'll put us in the next Great Mission movie!"

"If only," Elena said, and sat back in her chair, taking her hand away.

Just then Jimmi's dad came to the podium, and the assembly began.

Chapter Three
The Great Mission

Jimmi's dad stood in front of the giant screen. "Good morning, students and teachers."

"Good morning, Mr. Murphy," we said back.

"We are about to watch the history of our mission here to Perses. What Hans Melming dubbed the Great Mission."

Elena gave out an audible groan next to me. It was a risky move in a school where all the teachers knew what you sounded like.

My mother turned around and frowned at her. Elena gave her most innocent smile back.

"Shhhh," my mother said.

I shrugged and slid down in my seat.

My mother frowned at me, too, but turned back around.

Mr. Murphy had heard the complaint as well, but he held his hands up and nodded. "I know. This movie will be old news to many of you. But we at Melming Mining feel it is important to remind ourselves why we are here. Especially as we begin our first Blackout. So sit back and enjoy a history about the Earth, the human race, and your role in our Great Mission."

He bowed and walked off the stage.

"I don't know how you can find this boring," I whispered.

Elena leaned back in her seat and closed her eyes. "If I start snoring, jab me in the ribs before your mom catches me."

The lights dimmed.

The grainy image of a really old newscast filled the screen. A serious-looking woman stared at the camera and spoke.

"And before we go, one interesting little story from space. Scientists at the lunar observatory say they have discovered a large shadowy mass in the far reaches of our solar system."

An image of distant stars twinkled as the woman continued. I was mesmerized.

"Deep-space telescopes have observed a wobble in the orbits of the outlying satellites and asteroids in the Kuiper Belt, the band of floating matter and asteroids that sits outside the main planets of the solar system. It might sound like a Hollywood movie, but scientists say whatever it is, it poses a mathematically insignificant chance of ever impacting the Earth."

The image faded and was replaced by an image of children playing in a field of waving grass.

A man's voice spoke over the pictures.

"Earth was as close to paradise as it had been since the beginning of mankind's reign on the planet. Technology had solved many of the problems humans had been dealing with for centuries.

"Clean energy had cleared up the skies.

"Terra-forming, originally intended for space exploration, reclaimed farmland that had gone fallow, rivers that had run dry.

"With food, water, and shelter for all, war practically vanished from the Earth.

"Eden? Perhaps not, but it was a time of peace and plenty."

I mouthed along to the words. Elena leaned in close to me and whispered, "Whoever wrote this should have been sent on a one-way trip to Jupiter."

I ignored her.

A series of images passed across the screen as the man described all the wonders technology had brought to the world—solar energy, medical miracles, superfast computers.

Then dramatic music signaled a change in the story.

"For centuries miners had uncovered the minerals and nutrients that kept the whole system of civilization working smoothly. But resources are finite. Silicon, platinum, gold, silver, and titanium had been depleted.

"Crops failed.

"Technology failed.

"Earth was running out of the building blocks for life."

I shuddered each time I heard that line. We'd learned in school how war had returned in the fight for dwindling resources, how close the human race had come to destroying itself.

The screen was now filled with a view of the solar system.

"And then fate intervened, although no one could have foreseen the silver lining that would accompany the storm clouds."

There was a more modern news report. The newscaster's mouth was a thin line as she delivered her information.

"We have breaking news. Scientists at the Global Observatory in Oslo say Earth is in the path of a massive asteroid. How big and how much time will it take to reach Earth? They have named it Perses, after the ancient Greek god of destruction.

"We will have more details as they become available."

The screen showed a rapid-fire series of images as the object emerged from shadow into reflected sunlight. The closer it got, the more clearly scientists could gauge its size and shape. Then yet another news anchor appeared.

"Scientists say Perses is actually an enormous planetoid, and it is hurtling toward Earth. Perses doesn't

*need to directly strike the Earth to destroy everything.
If it passes close enough, its gravitational pull could rip
our atmosphere off like a sheet from a bed."*

The anchor ended the report by staring at the camera
in disbelief.

The voiceover returned.

*"The world was again united. United in fear, but
united in purpose. The world's best scientists gathered
in Norway to work together to try to save the Earth."*

A series of newspaper front pages twirled on the
screen with huge headlines.

SCIENTISTS: BLOWING UP PERSES WON'T WORK
NOT ENOUGH BOMBS TO BUDGE PERSES AN INCH
MOVE THE EARTH WITH A MASSIVE EXPLOSION?
SUICIDE, SAY TOP SCIENTISTS
PEOPLE URGED TO PRAY FOR A MIRACLE

My heart raced, knowing what was coming next.

The booming music ended, replaced by the sound
of boat horns, seagulls, and rocking waves. The camera
showed a young bearded man sitting on the edge of a

cliff, watching as boats came and left the docks below.

"The answer, in the end, was . . . tugboats.

"Hans Melming, a brilliant young scientist, knew time was quickly running out as Perses grew closer and closer to Earth. He decided to visit his beloved seashore, perhaps for the last time.

"As he sat on the cliff's edge, he watched tugboats moving huge transport tankers into the port."

Now there was a clip of an interview Melming had given a reporter a few years later, his beard now flecked with white.

"The tugboats are so tiny, they look like they should get crushed. But they use their smaller mass to tweak the movement of the bigger object ever so slightly. I instantly realized that the same approach would work in space. It had to do with gravity. The closer something is, the more its mass pulls on the objects around it."

"I'm not sure I totally understand," said the reporter.

Melming smiled like a kind uncle.

"Take Jupiter, for example. Jupiter is huge, but it's so

far away from the Earth that it has almost no gravitational effect on us at all.

"The Moon is miniscule in comparison, but because it's so close, it changes the Earth's orbit slightly and even sets the tides. See?"

The reporter nodded, and Melming continued.

"We couldn't move something as big as the Moon, but we could send small rockets into the asteroid belt, out past Mars. These rockets, targeted precisely, would move small asteroids, which would then move bigger asteroids and then even bigger asteroids, and so on and so on, until there was a kind of fleet of space rocks heading right for the flight path of Perses.

"The collective mass of all those rocks had a powerful gravitational pull, and they nudged Perses just enough to make the plan a success."

"To save the Earth, you mean," said the reporter. *"You are a hero."*

Melming smiled but shook his head. *"Those are very kind words. I am just a scientist who had a theory that worked in practice, that is all."*

The voiceover returned.

"There was one more miracle that even Melming had not anticipated. The Sun caught Perses in its orbit, pulling it into what is known as the habitable zone, not too hot or too cold for life.

"The Sun's heat melted the surface. There was water. Spectral examination showed Perses also had everything else the Earth desperately needed—minerals, nutrients, precious metals.

"Hans Melming founded a space exploration mining company, with invention after invention bringing the exploration of Perses closer to reality. Melming Mining is a nonprofit scientific company dedicated to providing equal resources to all the nations of Earth. The world's governments pledged their support to Melming's vision to mine Perses to save humanity. Hans Melming called this plan the Great Mission.

One last news report closed the movie. I always liked this one because it showed a picture of a little me, waving as we got into our shuttle to Perses. And my dad and mom even got interviewed.

A smiling reporter stood outside the launch pad.

"Melming Mining is about to launch the Great Mission—a manned mining colony on Perses. Terraforming has been in place for the past two years, making much of the surface habitable.

"A handful of brave men and women have signed on to help mine the resources of the planetoid for transport back to Earth. And families are more than welcome.

"James and Susan Nichols are even bringing their son along."

There was a close-up of my father.

"Melming Mining has a longer vision, settling Perses as a colony. So there are a number of families, like ours, who are coming. Happier employees are better employees."

My mom's face filled the screen.

"Besides, our son, Christopher, has wanted to go to space since the day he was born. I think he's more excited than we are!"

There was a close-up of me, beaming.

The reporter came back on-screen.

"Melming Mining expects it will take up to six years to make the colony fully operational and ready to send the first shipments home. One thing is for certain. Everyone on Earth is cheering for these brave men, women—and children—hoping the Great Mission is yet one more miracle."

There was a swell of music as the screen showed our shuttle blasting off into space.

The lights came back up in the auditorium.

My heart was racing. I wanted to pump the air with my fist and let out a loud whoop!

Mr. Murphy walked back to the podium.

"Now, that's why we are here. We are here to help. That means we need to be brave and we need to make sacrifices. I know that can sound a little frightening. But I have a surprise announcement that might make the Blackout a little less scary."

An electric murmur shot through the students.

"As you were making your way into the auditorium, more than a few people, managers, teachers, and even my son, Jimmi, approached me with a suggestion."

Elena turned to me, a huge grin spreading across her face.

We looked over at Jimmi, who was also grinning

from ear to ear. He looked at us and nodded. *"I rock,"* he mouthed.

"I have quickly conferred with my management team, and it has been decided that we should greet the arrival of the first Blackout of the Great Mission with a party."

Elena leaped up onto her chair seat and began whipping her hand over her head. "Yes! Yes!" she said.

My mother turned around quickly, motioning for Elena to sit down.

As Elena sat down, she slapped me on the shoulder. "A party! A real party! We did it!"

She gave me a high five, and then stared at me, eyes wide.

Mr. Murphy was announcing some of the possible plans, but Elena was just staring at me. It was making me feel uncomfortable.

"What? Do I have something on my face?"

She shook her head. "No. I was just thinking. This will be the first real party we've ever had up here."

"We've had birthday parties and stuff," I said, not getting it.

"Not the same thing. This is like a big New Year's Eve ball. This is special."

"And?"

"People go to parties like that *with* someone."

Elena's eyes stayed locked on mine, but she didn't say anything else. I was totally confused. Was she asking me out? Was she asking me to ask her out?

Did I want to ask her out? We were just friends, weren't we?

Why wasn't she saying anything?

Mr. Murphy's voice broke through the silence between us.

"But it takes a little research to put on a perfect party. So, we are giving you the rest of the school day to come up with some plans and suggestions for how to make this party, the Blackout Bash, the best party ever! To the library!"

There was a cheer from the students as they and the teachers got up and headed for the doors.

Finn, Alek, and the others all gave us thumbs-ups as they got out of their seats.

Elena began to stand up, her smile fading. She lowered her eyes from mine.

I stumbled around, trying to think of what to say. "I mean, we'll all be kind of going with everyone else in our class, won't we? Is that what you mean?"

"Yeah," she said. "I can't wait." Then she turned and joined the crowd.

"Wait, Elena!" I called, but Elena was now chatting

with Maria and Mandeep about what music they were going to request. Then they were gone.

I slumped back down in my seat. What the heck was going on?

My mother walked up the aisle and smiled at me. "I'm glad I had such a great idea."

I grinned but didn't say anything.

She sat down next to me.

"Everything good?" she asked.

I wanted to ask her for some advice, ask her what Elena might have been thinking. But when I looked at her, it just seemed too weird.

"No. I'm good," I said, standing up. "It's going to be a great party."

"I agree," she said. "And you better remember to suggest the fireworks."

We walked out of the auditorium together.

Chapter Four
Blackout Bash

The party started a few hours before the Earth said good-bye, or we said good-bye to the Earth. I guessed it depended on your perspective. The kids had made tons of suggestions, and Melming Mining, thanks to Mr. Murphy, had actually come through big time.

There were three big circles of tables taking up most of the field. Pavel's idea had expanded to include circles for the Earth and the Sun.

A set of tables sat at one edge of the field—the Earth. They were covered in layers of junk food, sugary drinks, cakes, pies, hot dogs. Those foods were rare on Perses. Usually, we got packaged stuff or vegetables. Space was not a place to be picky.

The Perses table was at the other end of the field, covered with presents for all the kids. There were even gold-wrapped parcels for older kids like Elena and me. I could tell ours were books by the way they were wrapped, which was great, but not as exciting to open as a toy ray gun or computer game.

And my dad had hinted that there was also a high likelihood of fireworks once the Sun went down.

The Sun was represented by a giant circle of tables in the middle of the field. That was where everyone was hanging out, sitting, eating, chatting, and, on a tempo-rary wooden platform in the middle, dancing.

There weren't a lot of people on Perses in total, and when we got together, you really noticed how few of us there were. Maybe a hundred. The ten farmers on Perses had come for the night, and they and the miners were mixing pretty comfortably with the brainiac scientists and the managers, like my dad.

Finn's idea for a big Blackout radio show had been worked out, and the DJs on the station were playing requests and sending messages to us from family back home.

"Aunt Cecilia says, 'Ti amo,' to Stefano Sebastiani. See

you in a couple of months!" Stefano was in the lower grade.

"Take care, Dan Huang. Love, your grandfather Luke."
Ditto for Dan.

"'Back in Black' from AC/DC is going out to Jennifer
Singh from her waiting fiancé, Gurdeep."

That one got a huge *"awww"* from the crowd, as
Jennifer, the other teacher up here, broke down in tears.
She'd put off her wedding to be on Perses, while her
fiancé waited until her three-year contract was done.

"This golden oldie goes out to all the hard workers
on Perses. It's 'Working in the Coal Mine' by Lee Dorsey!"

I kept looking for Elena. I saw her mom and dad,
but no sign of her. I had already looked in the likeliest
places—by the chips, the pop, the presents—but no Elena.

We hadn't talked much since the assembly. Every
time I tried to talk to her or hang out, she said she was
busy planning or hanging out with Maria and Mandeep
or Alek, making banners and decorations.

Giant banners with BRING ON THE BLACKOUT, or TTYL,
EARTH written in black paint hung around the field on
poles. I'd helped out with a few of them, but there'd
always been a bunch of us together.

There was a loud burst of static from the speakers,
and the music faded out and then came back. The noise
sent an excited buzz through the crowd.

The Blackout was getting closer and closer.

Even without Elena, I was enjoying the food. I was enjoying the music. I was enjoying the calculations I was doing in my head about how the Earth and Perses were revolving around the Sun.

I was even enjoying watching the miners sipping on bottles of some mysterious clear liquid. I had a pretty good idea that it was Perses-shine. Elena's father had told us there was a secret distillery hidden in the network of mines.

The miners got louder and louder, and once in a while would break out in rambunctious songs of their own, about life in the tunnels, or ballads to loved ones who had been left behind, buried in mines or back on Earth.

My dad joined in on more than a few and knew all the words. I caught him taking a swig from the bottles, and he and my mom even took a few turns on the dance floor together.

I watched as they spun and twirled, and was surprised by how well my dad could move despite his limp.

A punk rock song came on, and they sat down, my dad wincing a little, until someone passed him a bottle. He and my mom kissed, and with a gag I turned my attention back to the dance floor.

That was when I finally saw Elena—dancing, and not by herself.

She had her long black hair tied up in a ponytail that whipped around as she spun like a frenzied top. She was wearing a flower-print dress, but she had written *Bopping to the Blackout* across the top in some kind of paint or marker.

She was also wearing her favorite red army boots and black leggings.

She looked . . . cool.

I hadn't even thought to look for her on the dance floor. Who knew she liked to dance?

Brock, apparently, because he was doing his best to match her step for step. At one point they kicked at the same time, and he dinged her in the shins.

She laughed.

My stomach started to churn, and I put down the cupcake I'd been about to scarf.

I heard a shuffling, and my dad came over and sat down next to me. "Christopher, let's have a talk."

"Okay," I said. I couldn't take my eyes off the dance floor.

"I'm going to give you two pieces of advice." His voice was actually trembling a bit. I stole a peek at him. He was wringing his enormous hands together. "First of all I don't know what the next couple of months are going to be like, but I do know that we'll meet whatever challenges come up together as a family."

"Um, okay," I said. I didn't like the serious tone in his voice. He didn't sound like someone at a big fun party.

"Let's just say there are fail-safe measures, contingency plans. And there are other . . . things," he added cryptically. He seemed to be talking to himself now, more than to me.

"Okay," I said again, not quite sure what first bit of advice was hidden in this speech.

"Your mother and I would never have brought you here if we weren't sure this would be safe and secure. Space is not always the best place for kids. For kids . . ." He trailed off and rubbed his hands together again.

I touched his knee. He was worrying me. "Dad, you okay?"

He lifted his head and smiled. "Sorry, just a little tired. There's been a lot of long nights making sure we sent all the information to Earth and got everything locked down here for the Blackout."

I knew this was true. I'd barely seen him between the night we'd talked about my calculations and the night of the party.

He laughed suddenly. "And dancing with your mother— well, that will tire anyone out!"

That sounded more like my dad. He even looked over at Mom, who was chatting with Jennifer and passing tissues to her. She saw him and smiled.

He turned back to me slowly. "Christopher, this is an amazing party, so a huge thanks for suggesting the idea in the first place. And all I'm trying to say, despite my brain being on snooze, is that no matter what happens, you don't need to worry. That's advice number one."

"Okay. Thanks. I'm not that worried, actually. I'm kind of excited. I've even planned some experiments for school, plant growth and radiation levels, stuff like that."

"That's my son, the genius." He slapped my knee. "Okay, advice number two. Take charge. If you keep sitting here and watching that young lady dance, you'll keep watching until the Earth comes back. Go have fun."

He laughed and then stood up. I stayed frozen to the spot. I glanced at Elena. She was still spinning, although now with Alek.

My dad put a hand on my shoulder and pushed. I couldn't help but stand up. It was either that or fall flat on my face.

"Go. And. Have fun . . . Dance," he said, and there was the same tone he had in his voice when he ordered me to turn out the light at night or go to bed. It was not a tone that gave you the option for disagreement.

I shuffled in the direction of the dance floor. As I made my way closer, I ran through an itinerary of all the things that could go wrong. I checked my fly to make sure it was closed. I checked my armpits to make sure they didn't smell. I hoped my breath didn't smell too much like broccoli soup or cupcakes.

I took a panicked look down at my shirt. Had I dropped any icing down my front?

Before I knew it, I was on the dance floor, staring dumbly at Elena as she continued to dance up a storm. She spotted me and came over, smiling.

"Nice party!" Elena yelled over the music. She grabbed my arms and swung me into a spin. I wasn't sure if it was dancing or aerobics, but whatever it was, it was fun. I looked at Alek and Brock, who were frowning a bit at being shoved aside so easily.

I realized I didn't care.

The music crackled in the distance, drowned out by a burst of static.

We stopped spinning. Elena had to take a deep breath, and she laughed as she reached over and gave me a gentle punch on the arm.

"Christopher Nichols. You might be a geek, but you can actually dance!"

The radio came back to life.

"Whoa, almost time to say good-bye!" said the DJ. "Maybe time for one more tune. Here's Gustav Holst's love song to the planet Venus."

It was a slow song, a classical piece, with soaring flutes and strings. It sounded like a planet moving in the heavens.

Elena reached over and swung her arms around my shoulders.

"Hey, a slow song. Seems the perfect way to end this party."

"I'm not sure I know how to slow dance," I said.

"Ah, it's a cinch. Just try not to step on my feet! Maybe there's some mathematical schematic pattern thingy you can come up with."

"I'll do my best."

We danced for a bit, and I concentrated hard on where her feet and mine were, while Elena kept me from smashing into the other people on the floor.

"So, this party has been excellent," she said as we moved around the dance floor. "I've never danced so much in my life!"

"I was looking for you. I didn't even think to look on the dance floor."

"Well, now you know. I like to dance."

"I'm kind of liking it too."

She smiled at me, and I smiled back.

The static became more frequent, the music less and less clear, but we stayed together, dancing.

Somewhere above us, the Earth was sneaking behind the Sun.

I realized with a jolt I hadn't checked my watch to be sure my calculations were right.

I realized I didn't care about that, either.

Back at the tables, someone started a countdown.

"Ten, nine, eight, seven . . ."

Everyone joined in.

Elena smiled. "It *is* like a New Year's Eve party," she said.

"Six, five, four, three . . ."

"And, Christopher Nichols, you know what people do at exactly midnight on New Year's Eve?"

"Wear goofy party hats?"

"Two!"

She leaned in close and said in a whisper, "No."

"One!"

The music sputtered and died.

"Zero."

At that precise moment the Earth disappeared, and Elena Rosales leaned her lips toward me.

A huge crack and boom sounded from somewhere overhead.

Her lips drew closer.

"Fireworks," I said, unsure whether to turn and watch or let my best friend kiss me.

Then I heard screams.

Elena looked over my shoulder and gasped. I saw the panic in her eyes and turned around just as the first bombs fell.

Chapter Five

Battle

The world erupted around us. Everything was noise, fire, and chaos.

People ran in every direction, plowing into everyone else. The tables, the food, the presents were all in flames. Explosions tore apart the field. Chunks of singed grass and dirt flew into the air.

More bombs fell from the sky, obliterating everything and everyone on the ground.

I reached for Elena's hand, either to run away or maybe (if I give myself some credit) to run and help get people to safety, but as soon as I touched her fingers, a bomb exploded right next to us. The force threw me into the air. I landed with a thud in a cloud of dust and smoke.

I tried to stand, but I wobbled and fell over.

My hand was empty.

Clouds of smoke obscured the entire surface.

I called out for Elena. I couldn't hear my own voice. I called again, but still nothing. Elena was likely as deaf as I was.

Or maybe she had taken the brunt of the explosion.

The thought of her dead jolted me upright. I began to stumble, searching for any sign of her. I fell. I grew more and more desperate, blindly pawing the ground with my hands, then running around in circles.

I kept calling and shouting.

I tripped in a crater and hit my head on something hard—a rock or a chair or a person's boot.

I'm not even sure how long I was there before my eyes blinked open. All I saw was blinding light. It took me a moment to realize I was staring at the setting Sun. A dark shadow passed back and forth in front of it. Whatever it was, it was huge, and it was sending the bombs toward the field. Every bomb stoked the growing fire.

Something reached out of the light and lifted me up by the front of my shirt.

I shadowed my eyes and saw a face staring back at me through the smoke.

It was my father. He was mouthing something to me, shouting even, but I still couldn't hear.

I shook my head and pointed at my ears.

"I can't hear," I said. I must have shouted it, because my dad winced.

He gave up yelling, and grabbed my forearm. He began to walk away, dragging me behind, still dazed. I could see he was bleeding from his shoulder. His uniform was in tatters, and I could see his tattoo.

My forehead was throbbing. I touched it and realized I was bleeding too.

The field burned all around us. We headed for the roof of our building. I heard a ringing sound. It grew louder and, slowly, the sounds of the battlefield crept into my ears, more and more definite as our walk turned to a limping run.

I looked back. The shadow I'd seen in front of the Sun was a ship, and it was preparing to land. The bombs had stopped, replaced by energy-pulse bullets that sprayed into the crowd.

The bombs blew up anything they came near. These bullets were more accurate, targeted.

"Christopher!" I heard my mother's voice through the barrage. She was standing just to my left, bleeding from a gash on her head. She seemed to be holding an oddly shaped gun, firing brightly lit bursts back toward the ship.

I looked more closely at the gun my mother was holding and realized with a shock it was just a Roman candle, part of the fireworks from the party.

Completely useless.

Her eyes met mine. She shouted, "Run!" An energy bolt slammed into her, and she disappeared in a shower of flame and smoke. I blinked.

She was gone.

She was dead.

I tried to scream, but no sound would come out. I lunged toward the empty spot where she'd been standing seconds before.

"No," my father said, tightening his grip on my forearm. He continued to pull me toward our home. "We have to keep going." I started punching his arm to force him to let me go, but he was too strong. He ran faster, pulling me along as more energy pulses hit the ground around us, spraying debris everywhere.

We reached the core-scraper. Huge holes had been blasted in the roof, and acrid black smoke billowed out of the holes. The elevators, miraculously, were still working. One rose up, and the doors opened.

Dad dragged me inside and yelled, "Fifteenth floor!"

As the doors slid shut behind us, I saw that the ship had landed. Helmeted figures were emerging from landing stairs, firing more bursts.

The elevator shuddered as it descended, and the sounds of the battle faded.

Mom? I mouthed. My ears were still ringing, and the sound seemed deafening in the silence of the elevator.

My father's face was as still as stone.

I assume the tinny voiced woman in the elevator said, *"We have arrived at the fifteenth floor,"* but I don't remember.

The elevator doors opened, and my father led me into the hallway.

He took off one of his boots and jammed it between the elevator doors. The doors hit the boot and slid back open.

"Please allow the doors to close," said the woman. *"Please allow the doors to close. Please allow the doors to close."*

Dad ignored the voice and marched to our apartment. He kicked the door open so hard, the panels cracked and flew across the floor.

He led me to the table and sat me down. A loud boom echoed down the elevator shaft. All the lights flickered.

"We don't have much time," he said as he began rummaging through our bookshelves.

I sat, immobile.

My father threw a whole row of books off the shelf. They landed with a crash on the floor. He grabbed something that had been tucked behind the books, a small backpack. He marched back to the table.

"Take this," he said. I didn't move. He took my hand and wove the backpack strap in between my fingers. It felt weightless, empty, and I was clearly confused.

"Inside is a map. Repeat after me: a map."

I nodded. "A map." He began to search for something else, tossing books everywhere.

My brain started to unfreeze. "A map for what?"

He didn't answer right away. "Got it," he said finally, turning around.

He was holding a gun.

"Christopher, you can't stay here. You need to get some food and water and get yourself into that elevator and go to the mines. Fill up your backpack."

He motioned to the kitchen cupboards.

I didn't move. "Wait, what? You're going back?" I said. "No, you can't. You can't."

He took my shoulders in his hands and stared right into my eyes. "Christopher. You need to be strong.

You need to survive. I've got to go back."

I shook my head. Tears began to fill my eyes.

He took a deep breath. "I am going back to fight. Maybe I, maybe we adults, can buy some time."

I shook my head. "Let me fight with you."

"No, you have another job. There are children, survivors, who are going to need you. Head down the mines and keep them safe."

"No!"

"You have to."

"No!"

"There's no other choice. None. Do you understand?" He didn't let go of my shoulders until I nodded, the tears returning.

He grabbed the bag from my lap and held it up in front of my eyes. "In here there is a map. It is your only chance to be rescued. Repeat that after me."

"My only chance," I said.

"Your mother . . . ," He choked on the words for a second. "She and I and some of the miners hid an emergency beacon where no one could find it."

"An emergency . . . what? What do you mean you hid it?"

"Susan, your mother, she and I have always been wary. Wary and worried."

I just stared back at him.

He sighed. "I don't have time to explain it all. Humans are complex. We've always told you we were convinced of the worthiness of this mission. We came to Perses to do great things."

I nodded.

"But power, money . . . Those do funny things to people. We, your mother, me, Elena's father, we all knew there was a chance, a small chance, that things might not work out so well. We knew we might need a backup plan."

There was another large boom, and the lights flickered again. Cracks began to appear in the ceiling above the table.

"I don't know what's going on up top," he continued, "who those monsters are, but there are people on Earth who are watching for any sign of trouble. You'll need to survive the Blackout and signal them for help."

The tears were now rolling down my face.

He held up a black flashlight. "You'll need this to read the map." He tossed the flashlight into the bag.

"Why can't you just tell me where the beacon is?" I choked on tears.

"It's very complicated. I'm not even sure I *could* tell you. Everything you need to figure it out is there."

"Where?" I said.

Another, bigger boom rattled the building. The cracks in the ceiling and the walls splintered and grew.

"No more time to waste. Stand up." He said it in his authoritative voice. I stood up.

My dad stuffed the backpack full of food and water, then grabbed my arm and hurried me back to the elevator. He handed me the backpack.

"Dad, I . . . I can't . . ."

"No more talking." He leaned in and hugged me and then stepped back into the hallway. He bent down and grabbed his boot.

"Seventy-fifth floor," he said. "Manager override. Floor fifteen now closed."

"Affirmative," said the woman.

The doors to the elevator began to close. My dad smiled and waved, like I was going away on a school bus.

"If I can, I will find you," he said.

Then he got a surprised look on his face, like he'd suddenly remembered something. The elevator doors closed completely, and I began to descend.

"Christopher, the map is—" but there was another huge blast, and the sound drowned out his words.

I don't know what the last bit was he meant to say.

I never got another chance to ask.

Chapter Six
Orphaned

I slumped against the back wall of the elevator as it descended lower and lower toward the bottom of the core-scraper. I wanted to order the doors to reopen, to let me get out and join my dad, or maybe to die fighting with him.

But I didn't. I couldn't. My dad had given me an order.

Why did he go back?

He was going to buy us time, he said.

Us.

What did that mean?

As the floors passed, more questions joined the ones already in my head.

Who would want to attack us?

Why?

Was I an orphan?

My mother had been killed right before my eyes. My father was heading back to the surface to fight . . . who? Pirates? Terrorists? Soldiers? Armed people with guns way bigger than the tiny pistol he'd grabbed from the bookcase. He knew he was going to die and he knew I knew.

Was Elena dead too?

What was the point of surviving if my parents, if Elena, weren't there anymore?

Why would I want to live if everyone I cared about was gone?

I slammed my fist onto the floor.

The pain just made me more furious.

I slammed my hand down again and again and again.

Then I remembered dancing with Elena, her hands in mine, her face drawing toward mine just before the bombs separated us from each other.

I stopped punching the floor.

I did need to go back. I needed to find my father, to find Elena. Dead or alive.

Whoever needed help would have to help themselves. I was about to tell the elevator to head back to the surface when I heard a sound.

Sobbing.

It was just as I passed the twenty-eighth floor.

"Stop!" I yelled.

The elevator jolted to a stop.

"Twenty-eighth floor, and hurry!

The elevator began to rise when one more bang shook the building. The lights flickered on and off.

I could hear loud pings as something fell on top of the elevator, like pebbles. The roof must have been hit and was collapsing. The lights came back on, and the elevator rose again. I could hear the cries getting louder.

"We have arrived on the twenty-eighth floor," said the voice.

The doors opened just as a giant chunk of something smashed into the top of the elevator. The force threw me to the floor. I looked up. The ceiling was dented and bent in at the edges, like someone had stepped on top of a pop can.

The brakes squealed as the elevator tried to hold its position in the shaft. Whatever was on top was heavy.

I scrambled to my feet and stuck my head through the opening. The elevator had already slipped about a foot below the level of the floor.

Dark smoke thickened in the hallway, making it

difficult to see. I looked up and down the hallway for the source of the sobbing.

Leaning in a doorway a few feet away was Darcy Aveline, five years old. She was clutching a stuffed dog, crying. I wasn't sure why she was down here alone. I'd seen Darcy's parents blown up in the first attacks.

She stared at me, and her eyes grew wide. She stopped crying, but she didn't move.

"Don't be afraid," I said. I was afraid. More smoke was rising up from the stairway door at the end of the hallway. I knew from our safety classes that smoke was just as deadly as fire, if not more so, and in about a minute Darcy would be overwhelmed. The elevator was our only hope to get out, and there was no way to stop it from sinking.

"Darcy," I said, trying to sound calm, all the while holding the doors open with my shoulders. "It's me, Christopher. Come on over. It's going to be okay. We're going to go down to the basement to play."

I smiled. I hoped she couldn't hear the panic in my voice as the elevator continued to slide. There was now just about a three-foot opening, and it was getting smaller and smaller.

"Darcy, we'll have fun. We're going on a treasure hunt!" I said. I reached into my backpack and pulled out a chocolate bar. "Look, I even took some treats from the party! But we have to hurry or everyone else will find the treasure first!"

Darcy started to get up.

The elevator lurched. There was now just two feet between the top of the door and the top of my head. "Darcy, come on over. Hurry."

I waved the chocolate bar back and forth. She was still walking too slowly.

Darcy continued to clutch the stuffed toy dog as she made her way closer and closer. The elevator was slipping. In just seconds there'd be no room left to save her.

"Darcy! HURRY!" I yelled. She stopped. I'd spooked her. *Idiot*, I said to myself.

She started to shake, and the tears welled in her eyes again. She took a step backward. One more step and she'd be lost.

I wasn't letting someone else die.

I grabbed the doors with my hands and hurled myself out. I hooked my feet on the doors to stop from flying out completely. Luckily for me, Darcy was so shocked, she stopped.

As I lunged, I reached out and grabbed her leg.

She screamed and started to wriggle, but I held tight. She fell over.

"Darcy, we need to go!"

The doors now slammed into my ankles, then reopened. I ignored the pain and pushed and pulled my body back across the floor, dragging Darcy along. I could hear the groaning of the elevator.

I had to be fast. The doors smashed my knees and reopened again. I desperately pushed with my free hand to send us into the elevator.

The elevator creaked. I pushed and pushed on the smooth concrete floor. I could feel the backpack rub against the top of the elevator doorway.

Finally my legs dangled down, and the weight of my lower body pulled us through.

I fell back and pulled Darcy with me, just as the elevator lurched and dropped below the floor. Darcy landed on my chest and knocked all the air out of my lungs.

I gasped for breath, and Darcy continued to scream.

But we were alive.

Her stuffed dog wasn't so lucky. One arm had been caught in between the floor and the elevator and was torn off completely.

Darcy stared at the dog. She screamed louder and hugged it close.

I gained my breath and then sat up. I hugged her.

"It'll be okay," I said. "We just needed to get away."

She was shaking.

"Elevator, slowly head to the seventy-fifth floor please."

The elevator headed down the shaft again, but not as slowly as I'd hoped. The brakes slowed us, but the growing weight of the debris on the roof threatened to send us crashing down.

Darcy held her dog and started talking between sobs.

"Friendly wanted to come to the party. Mom told me no. But when they were dancing, I came down to get him. Then there was a thunderstorm and smoke, and then I got scared. I was all alone."

I hugged her again. She didn't know how alone she was. How alone we all were.

"We'll be okay," I said. "We'll be okay."

As we descended, I listened as carefully as I could at every floor to see if anyone else was crying, or screaming or pounding or trying to hail the elevator.

I wouldn't risk stopping the elevator again, but if I could figure out the floors with children or survivors, I could come back later.

I didn't hear anyone.

"You have arrived at the seventy-fifth floor," the voice said.

The doors opened but jammed halfway, the top of the panels grinding against the sagging ceiling.

The hall was glowing red, and for a second I was afraid the room was on fire. My eyes adjusted. The only light came from the red emergency lights on the floor and ceiling.

The blasts from above must have triggered the seismic sensors in the floor, sending the tunnels into safety mode.

The elevator creaked.

I quickly ushered Darcy out into the hall. I could feel her tense as we walked into the semidarkness.

The light from the elevator spread out only a small bit, and it was flickering as more and more debris fell from the shaft.

I pulled out the flashlight my father had given me and flicked it on. No light. I shook it, but the light didn't come on.

I stared at the bulb, which now seemed to be glowing faintly, but not enough to be useful.

"Dead batteries. Great," I muttered. I flicked it off and tossed it back into my bag.

Luckily, I knew my way around.

The ceiling of the elevator groaned ominously. Another large chunk of concrete smashed into the roof.

I grabbed Darcy's hand.

"Let's go exploring," I said in as cheery a voice as I could muster.

Darcy held on to my hand, and we began to walk slowly into the gloom. She continued to grip her dog, bits of stuffing falling out of the empty arm socket.

I held my breath as we passed under the teeth of the blast door, looking even more like a mouth in the eerie red light.

"Is anyone there?" I called as loudly as I dared.

I could hear shuffling and sniffling coming from the darkness up ahead.

"It's okay," I called. "It's me, Christopher. Darcy is with me."

"And Friendly," Darcy said.

"Yes, all three of us are here, and I have some food and some water."

"And some chocolate," Darcy added.

A light shot up ahead, and a figure stepped out from the shadows. Instinctively, I pushed Darcy behind me.

It was Alek. He was holding a freshly lit flare and was shuffling toward me. He looked horrible, his face cut and scarred, bloodstains all over his shirt and pants. He took one more step, then teetered and fell over with a sickening thud. The flare skidded away on the floor toward the lockers.

I ran and grabbed it before it could catch anything on fire, and then held it high in the air.

The flare illuminated the terrified faces of a handful of my classmates: Finn, Jimmi, Mandeep, Pavel, and Maria. They huddled together against the lockers, some burying their faces in the uniforms.

There were no adults.

I held the flare higher, desperately looking for more faces, more kids, anyone.

Elena.

Elena wasn't there.

Maria's little sister wasn't there.

There were no other kids Darcy's age.

Maria saw Darcy, then began shaking her head, tears pouring down her face. "No, no, no," she said. She slid down to the floor and buried her head in her hands. The others just rocked back and forth, not moving, not talking.

I heard my father's voice. *There will be survivors. Keep them safe.*

I knelt down to check Alek's pulse. He was still alive, but covered in blood.

I took a deep breath.

"Okay, everyone. We need to get Alek to the infirmary. We need to find food, water, and shelter."

No one moved. Finn pushed his face farther into the fabric of the uniforms.

The uniforms. That gave me an idea. At the top of each locker was a helmet, and each helmet had a battery-powered light.

Light wouldn't make the situation any less serious. But it might help everyone feel less scared, myself included. I grabbed a uniform and laid it over the top of Alek's injured body.

Then I ran over and grabbed a helmet and put it on. I flicked the switch on the front, and the room was suddenly bathed in light—at least the parts I pointed my head at. I took another one and put it on Darcy. Just to help lighten the mood, I even gave her one for Friendly.

"Friendly likes his helmet," she said.

"That's good. Now tell him we're going on that treasure hunt."

"He likes treasure, too!" Darcy said, actually jumping up and down.

Somehow, the light and Darcy's enthusiasm seemed to focus everyone.

Mandeep reached up and grabbed a helmet from the locker behind her. She put it on Maria and adjusted the straps.

The helmets were way too big for most of us, but the

distraction of trying to stuff socks and shirts under the cap to hold them in place took everyone's mind off the immediate danger. We still weren't talking, but we were moving.

I could hear pings of more debris on the nearby elevators, and the smell of smoke grew stronger. We needed to move farther down the hall.

I turned back to Darcy. "I even have a secret map!" I said. "But I need some help getting sleepyhead over there. . . ."

"He's not sleeping. He's hurt," said Darcy.

"Yes. That's true. He's hurt. But there's a place down that tunnel where he can get better. And he does need to sleep. I just need some help to get him there safely."

"This might help." I turned to see Finn holding a tarp toward me. "We can put it under him."

I smiled and put a hand on his shoulder. "Thanks," I said.

Mandeep joined us. "I've seen my mom do this for emergency demonstrations." We carefully slid the tarp under Alek, lifting his legs and shoulders as gently as we could.

Then we each grabbed a corner and started walking down the hallway.

"Does anyone know a good song we can sing for our

adventure?" I called out, again trying to sound cheerful.

Finn looked at Darcy and whispered something. "The one with the dwarves!" she called.

"Perfect! Heigh-hooooooo!" I said, and started marching ahead, gingerly keeping Alek's head steady.

The elevator behind us collapsed under the weight of the concrete.

Darcy and the others turned around to look. I just belted out, "It's off to work we goooooooooooooooooo!" even louder.

Chapter Seven
Aftershock

Alek, it turned out, wasn't as injured as he looked, at least not physically. He had gashes and burns on his face and arms, but these were pretty easy to clean up with the bandages and gauze in the infirmary.

That was the good news.

The awful part was that this meant most of the blood on his shirt wasn't his.

Alek woke up almost as soon as we put him on a cot, but he didn't say anything. There was a poster on the wall of the infirmary that showed a smiling miner in a hardhat, along with the slogan WE ARE WHAT MAKES MELMING MINING GREAT. WE ALL WORK TOGETHER.

He just stared at the poster, rarely even blinking. He

did moan once when I bumped into his ankle—it was hard moving a patient in a mostly dark room—but that was the only noise he seemed able, or willing, to make.

Mandeep dressed the cuts on Alek's head and put disinfectant on the rest of his wounds. She clumsily strapped a brace from one of the cupboards onto his ankle so he could walk.

"I think that's how my mom does . . . I mean, did that," she said, lowering her head.

We would have to walk eventually. Maybe sooner than we wanted. How much longer before the attackers started searching for survivors?

But right now it was the middle of the night, and what we all needed was rest.

Luckily, Darcy had fallen asleep, tucked up on a pile of uniforms on the infirmary floor, clutching Friendly in her arms. Mandeep had bandaged him up too.

Finn was asleep on the other cot. He'd cried himself to sleep, murmuring the names of his parents.

The others were leaning on the walls outside the infirmary, barely conscious of what was going on. The red emergency lights kept everything in a kind of surreal gloom.

I asked Mandeep to join me a little farther down the hallway.

"We need to start thinking about a plan," I said.

"What everyone really needs is to get some rest," she said.

I nodded. "I agree. I just meant that you and Finn and I are the only ones who are even talking. Everyone else is walking around like a bunch of zombies."

"Can you blame them?"

I wasn't choosing my words very well. "I'm sorry. I'm not trying to . . . It's just that I think we need to get everyone talking."

"Talking? Seriously?" She was annoyed.

"Yes, talking. It will actually help."

"How do you know that?"

"The year my grandpa died . . . It was right before we moved to Perses. We were really close, but he'd lost his memory near the end. He kept referring to me as his long-lost brother, Ned. He died not even remembering who I was. That was hard. But what my parents always did, through all of this, was talk. They'd ask me questions about what I was thinking or what I was feeling."

Mandeep relaxed her shoulders. I continued.

"Sometimes we'd just talk about nothing stuff, the weather or books, or the latest video game. It helped. We didn't pretend Grampa wasn't sick; they just didn't let it become the only thing we talked about."

Mandeep nodded. "Okay. Maybe that's a good idea, but it's going to be rough."

"I know," I said. "For all of us."

Mandeep nodded, her eyes tearing up.

I walked up to Jimmi, Pavel, and Maria. Maria was still rocking back and forth on the floor, holding her knees in her arms.

Pavel seemed to be punching the wall, his knuckles raw and bloody.

"Anyone want a chocolate bar?" I said. I pulled a few out of my backpack and waved them around. "I grabbed a bunch on my way down."

Maria stopped rocking and looked at me, her teeth gritted. "Are you joking?" she said. "My family, my sister . . . they're all—"

"Dead," I said, bowing my head. "I know. I saw my mom get killed. My dad is probably dead too. All of us"—I paused, to stop myself from crying—"all of us are alone now. *We* are all we have. And if we want to make it, if want to live we have to . . . to . . ." One of Elena's favorite phrases, in her own voice, came to me. "We need to kick ourselves in our own freaking butts."

"My sister isn't dead!" Maria said, shaking. "She's still up there with my mom and dad. They're coming back for me."

She knew better, but I let her say it anyway. It was no good having an argument.

"My dad *is* dead," I said, knowing it was true. "And so is my mom. Whoever attacked us wasn't out to take prisoners."

We sat in silence for a long time after that. Then Jimmi said something that hit me like punch in the chest.

"You know, Nichols. Your dad and mom might be dead, but they were real heroes."

Pavel stopped punching and turned to me, nodding, the light on his helmet bobbing. "My mom died shielding me and Jimmi from a bomb hit. I couldn't move. Your dad grabbed us and threw us into the elevators."

"He took a chunk of something right in the leg, shrapnel or something. But he kept going back looking for kids."

"Alek was just wandering around up there. He was a sitting duck. Your mom led him through the smoke to the roof. She did the same for Finn and Mandeep."

"We're alive down here because of them."

I couldn't speak. I let images sink in. What would they do if they were still here?

"Thanks. That means a lot." A lump rose in my throat, but I forced it down. "But do you know what they'd say right now? They'd say we have to think about each other.

We're a family. If there are parents alive, and let's hope that's true, then we need to stay alive to help them, so they can find us. But if we are alone, we have to work together."

Their headlamps nodded in agreement.

"So what do we do now?" asked Maria.

"Should we run?" Mandeep asked.

"Should we try to go back up top?" Pavel asked. "I'd love to punch one of those . . ." he didn't finish but went back to hitting the wall.

"Yeah, should we fight?" Jimmi asked, reaching over and grabbing Pavel's arm before he could throw another punch.

They were all looking at me for answers. "We rest. Jimmi, you and I can take the first watch. Everyone else, try to get some sleep. There are enough uniforms down here to bunch up as beds and pillows."

"Maria and I will go get them," Mandeep said.

I gave a quick nod. "Try to keep close together, and be ready to move at a moment's notice. Jimmi and I will wake you if we see anything."

Jimmi and I set ourselves up by the blast door, and listened.

Ten minutes into the watch, Jimmi had fallen asleep.

I was alone with my thoughts. Elena's voice, the

image of my mom dying, and the new image of my mother and father being heroes . . . It was all too much. The sadness began to overwhelm me.

I put my backpack on my lap and began to rummage through it. I hadn't told anyone about the map or the beacon. Not yet. Once I'd read the map and come up with a plan and a direction to go, I'd get everyone's input.

The chocolate bars were the first things I pulled out. There were only ten or so, along with some energy bars my dad had thrown in. I laid them out on the floor.

Breakfast.

There would be more food down here, if it wasn't spoiling with the main power off. I knew there was a cafeteria not far down Tunnel 1 that served lunches when the miners were on long shifts. I'd also look for that break room in Tunnel 2. We'd head there in the morning. I'd try to convince Alek to make the trip with us.

I took out the flashlight and flicked it on. The light was still pathetic. I banged it in my palm just in case there was a loose connection in the bulb or the battery pack. No difference. I wasn't sure how I could recharge it. My dad hadn't given me a charging cord.

I put it back in the backpack and reached in for the map.

There was nothing in the main pouch. I started patting the sides. In the back of the pouch there was a kind of hidden pocket, held closed by a clasp.

I undid the clasp and pulled out a thin red, leather-covered book.

And that was it. The backpack was now empty.

I held the book up and shone my headlamp at it.

Oliver Twist by Charles Dickens.

Oliver Twist? I shook the book but nothing fell out. I flipped through the pages. It was just a book, a normal book.

In a panic I ran my hands through the backpack. I held it upside down and shook it. I even turned it inside out.

Empty.

The fabric was just plain cloth, no map drawn on it or woven into it.

My heart was racing. My dad had given his life so I'd be able to find the beacon. And I'd lost the map? Had it fallen out when I was saving Darcy? If it was in the elevator, it was gone. The compartment was crushed. There was no finding anything in there.

I looked back at the book.

Why give me a book? Why this book?

I shook it again. I flipped through all the pages again. It was just a book.

I was so angry and frustrated that I grabbed the front cover and tried to rip it off.

Then I saw the handwritten inscription on the front page.

> To Susan,
> A gift for you and our new baby boy.
> Read it to him at bedtime.
> When he's ready.
> Jim

I ran my fingers over the script.

Tears ran down my cheeks. My chest heaved with sobs. Had my dad wanted me to have the book as well as the map? Was that a final gift? Was this backpack kind of a treasure chest? I wanted him there so badly right now to explain what was going on, to tell me what to do next.

I held the book against my chest, hugging it. I'd come so close to throwing it away.

Jimmi stirred a few feet away from me.

"You cool?" he asked, sleepily.

"Yeah," I croaked. "Just bagged and sad and mad."

I wiped the tears from my eyes and tried to avoid the light from Jimmi's helmet.

"I hear that. Look, I caught some sleep," he said. "You get a few winks and I'll keep watch."

"Cool." I flicked off my helmet light. At least he hadn't seen me bawling my eyes out.

I carefully placed the book back in the pocket of the backpack, bunched up some uniforms on the floor next to me, and fell asleep.

Chapter Eight

Food Fight

Jimmi's snores woke me up not long after. I flicked on my headlamp and checked my watch. It was morning, early morning. Jimmi had three empty chocolate bar wrappers on the ground next to him. I frowned. We needed to ration the food, not devour it. Jimmi had had his breakfast; now I needed to make sure everyone else got some too. I stood up, stretched, and walked back toward the infirmary.

The red emergency lights kept everything lit like some kind of haunted house. The batteries in our helmets were only going to hold their charge for so long before they died. I needed to get the main lights back. There was probably a central panel or something that turned off the emergency system and rebooted the central lighting. I just needed to find it.

Mandeep was asleep in the hall outside the infirmary, wrapped up in a pile of uniforms. I tiptoed past her.

I heard whispered voices as I opened the infirmary door.

Maria was trying to calm Darcy, who'd woken up in a panic.

"I want my daddy and mommy," Darcy said, hugging Friendly so hard, she was practically crushing him.

Maria looked exhausted, but she was trying to soothe Darcy with cooing sounds and pats on the back. "It's okay, Isabel . . . Darcy." She choked up on saying the name of her little sister, and had to turn away.

Finn was sitting up in his bed, looking dazed. Alek was still on his side, staring blankly at the poster.

Pavel was standing against the wall, his hands in his pockets, looking annoyed by the whole scene.

Darcy saw me and jumped up from her bed. She rushed over, hugging my legs so hard, she almost toppled me over. "Christopher, where is my family?" She pointed at Finn. "When he was sleeping, he kept talking, and he said his daddy and mommy are dead."

Pavel gave a snort and smirked. "Pathetic," he said. He walked past me and out the door.

Finn looked shocked. "I didn't . . . I don't want to scare . . . I . . ." Then he just shook his head, his bottom lip trembling so much, he couldn't talk.

"It's okay, Finn," I said. "It's okay." Maria walked over and hugged him. They held each other silently.

I knelt down and looked straight into Darcy's eyes. "I know this is scary. I'm not going to lie to you. I don't know where our parents are."

Her lip trembled, but I continued.

"That thunderstorm you heard wasn't a real storm. It was an attack. People attacked us."

Darcy narrowed her eyes and frowned. "You mean like pirates?"

I nodded. "Yes. I think. I'm not sure. They dropped bombs. All of us down here in the mines, we are the only ones who I'm sure are alive."

Darcy hugged Friendly and took this in. "I hate them," she said at last. Then she turned and ran and tucked herself down into a corner of the room. "I hate them!" she screamed.

Maria and Finn continued to hold each other.

Pavel was probably outside punching the walls again.

Alek was comatose.

Mandeep appeared at the doorway, groggy and

rubbing her eyes. "I *just* got to sleep. Can't anyone shut up for a moment?" Then she turned back to the hallway and slammed the door.

I hung my head. How was I supposed to help get everyone through this? I had a hard enough time talking to people when things were normal.

Elena had been different.

She listened to me no matter what stupid thing I said.

But Elena was dead.

I had to do something. If we all sat around stewing in our grief, we'd never survive the Blackout.

I walked over to Darcy. "Hey, you know what I need right now?"

Darcy looked up at me and shook her head.

"I need a brave girl to help me find the light switch for down here. And we need to go find some food. There's a cafeteria down the tunnel with lots of chocolate and desserts. You want first dibs?"

Darcy nodded.

I smiled and held out my hand. She gripped it tightly, and we walked toward the door.

Finn raised his head off Maria's shoulder.

"Can I come?" Finn said.

I looked down at Darcy and raised an eyebrow. She nodded.

"Okay," I said. "But Darcy still gets first dibs on the desserts."

Finn gave a quick smile and joined us, wiping his eyes and nose on his sleeve.

"Maria, you want to come too?" I asked.

She shook her head and crawled onto the cot, pulling the sheets up over her head.

Well, at least the younger kids are moving, I thought.

We walked past Mandeep and Pavel, both sleeping or trying to, and headed toward the entrance to Tunnel 1. Finn was quietly humming the "Heigh-Ho" song. Darcy noticed too and joined in.

The sides of the tunnels were incredibly smooth. The ceilings arched above us about ten feet high in an almost perfect semicircle.

I marveled at this underground world. Diggers had carved out small exploration shafts with excavators following, carving out the full tunnel and then using shovel-arms to grab copper, iron . . . whatever.

For really precious metals—like gold or titanium—or jewels, they used something called a grinder. I'd never seen one, but I'd picked up from bits of conversation that these machines could get into small cracks and holes the bigger machines would destroy.

Just beyond the entrance to the tunnel, we came to a

large door with *cafeteria* spray painted on it. Someone with a sense of humor had added *Abandon all hope ye who enter here* in marker across the top.

The door wasn't locked, and cool air greeted us as we pushed the door open and walked inside. There were more motivational posters up on the walls, with slogans like FOOD AND WATER ARE AS PRECIOUS AS GOLD, DON'T WASTE, and REUSE AND RECYCLE.

The fridges and freezers were still working, so that meant there had to be some emergency batteries or power cells somewhere down here.

I tried the stoves, but they didn't ignite. Keeping food from spoiling was a priority; cooking it was apparently a luxury. So it was going to be raw veggies and salads until we got some actual power down here.

I turned on the taps and water flowed out. I quickly shut it off. Who knows how much clean water was left. The ponds up top were probably polluted from the battle, and I didn't want to think too much about that.

As promised, Darcy got to choose first and elected for an entire chocolate custard pie. I noticed the pie had been made on Earth in a place called Brighton, Ontario.

I'd never even heard of it, but a pang of homesickness still hit me.

Finn grabbed a chocolate bar and happily munched

away. "This is what I needed!" he said. "You want some?" He thrust the bar in my direction.

"No, I'm good. But don't eat too much. We do need to save some for the others."

Finn smiled and took another bite.

We completely inventoried all of the food in the fridges and on the shelves. There wasn't as much as I'd hoped. Worst-case scenario, we'd need food for three months: two until the Blackout ended, and then a month or so until we got rescued. There was nowhere near enough food down here to last that long, even with rationing.

Darcy grabbed another piece of pie, giggling as she pretended to share it with Friendly. Finn sat down next to her and opened yet another wrapped candy bar. The rationing could start tomorrow.

My parents' voices rang in my ears: my father ordering me to be a leader, my mother telling me to run. They both wanted me to survive. That meant staying underground. It was still dark, but now we had some food. If we were lucky, we could stay put and ride out the Blackout. Then we'd signal Earth and get saved. I didn't have it all worked out yet, but one thing we had was time.

"Okay, guys, let's grab some veggies and head back to camp."

"Aww," whined Darcy and Finn together.

"And make sure you wash the evidence off your hands and faces. I don't need everyone demanding dessert before breakfast!"

They got up, and we grabbed some food and headed back. I did stash some treats in my bag.

Mandeep and Pavel were up. Jimmi had woken up too but was still yawning as he leaned against the wall, stretching.

"I'm sorry," Mandeep said as we approached. "That wasn't really like me to yell like that."

"It's all good," I said.

Darcy hugged Mandeep and nestled into her arms tightly.

Finn and I passed out fresh beans and carrots to everyone. Alek and Maria were still sleeping, so I set theirs aside.

"Beans and carrots?" Pavel said, sticking out his tongue. "What, no Brussels sprouts left for dessert?"

I frowned. "Look. The fresh stuff, like the carrots, needs to be eaten first. There's not a lot of extra anything, and we can't afford to waste. Food is like gold for us, unless we can find some more, we have to get by with what we have."

Pavel scoffed but took a giant bite out of his carrot and sat, chewing it loudly.

But then I pulled out a box of chocolate bars. "If we eat our veggies, we'll get a treat."

Jimmi reached out, but I grabbed his hand before he could take one.

"After the veggies," I said.

He was ticked. "Who died and made you king?" he said under his breath.

I started to say, *My dad,* when I remembered he'd lost his family too.

"Never mind. Sorry. Just grab one."

"No, thanks. I don't want it anymore," Jimmi said, stomping away.

I walked into the infirmary Maria woke up and crunched on her veggies. She stared at the chocolate bar for a long time, then slid it into her pocket.

"It was Isabella's favorite kind," she said. But she got up and walked outside to join the others.

Alek was in worse shape. I offered him chocolate and water, but the food stayed in the wrapper, and the water trickled down the sides of his mouth.

He just stared straight ahead, barely even blinking.

Three nights in, nothing had changed. I was on watch duty alone. I settled into a comfortable spot on a corner of the locker room, and pulled out the copy of *Oliver*

Twist. I hoped reading it might help calm me and help me remember happier times with my mom and dad and their newborn baby boy.

I hadn't even cracked the spine when I heard a trickle of debris falling down the shaft of the ruined elevator. The bits pinged the sides on the way down and bounced off the remains of the elevator at the bottom. I put my hand on the ground to see if there were any tremors that might have dislodged some of the rubble.

Nothing. The floor was cool and calm.

I stashed the book in my backpack and walked over to the elevators. More pebbles or bits of whatever trickled down.

Then I heard a sound that sent a chill down my back.

One of the working elevators began to ascend back up its shaft.

Chapter Nine
Scorched Perses

Someone was at the other end of that elevator shaft. That was certain.

I did some quick calculations.

The chances that it was one of our parents or more kids making their way down to the basement couldn't be discounted. If that were the case, we should stay here and wait. That was my hope, the story I wanted to tell myself.

But I knew the concrete facts were against me. The debris that had crushed my elevator compartment that first day had been smoky and burning. That meant it had been freshly blasted, which meant the battle had reached the roof of the core-scraper just minutes after my father had left me.

The tremendous blasts had ended while I was saving Darcy, which meant the battle was over. I knew who had won that.

So the chance that it was one of our attackers in the elevator, getting ready to descend into the core-scraper to look for survivors, was *far* greater. And the chance that they wanted to keep those survivors alive? Zero.

We had to get away.

And we didn't have a lot of time.

I hustled back to camp. Mandeep and Maria were the first ones I saw, so I shook them awake. I tried to sound calm, but I could hear my voice rising to a high-pitched squeak.

"They're coming after us. We've got to get moving."

It didn't take a room light to see the panic in their eyes.

"Now," I said, firmly.

They scrambled to their feet.

"Gather as much food and water as you can."

"What about you?" Maria asked.

"I have a plan."

I actually didn't have a plan yet, but I quickly ran back to the locker room as one began to take shape.

I passed a storage locker filled with detonator caps and stopped. I remembered a book Elena had once read to me about something called the Russian Campaign of

1812. Napoleon, one of Elena's favorite historical nut-jobs, was attacking Russia. Instead of staying and fighting, the Russians retreated but burned everything first, making sure Napoleon wasn't able to salvage anything he could use to help his troops or attack. *Scorched-earth policy*, she'd called it.

Napoleon eventually ran out of supplies.

The Russians won.

Running wasn't enough. I needed to make sure they couldn't get at anything they could use to follow us. I stared at the teeth of the blast door.

I needed to figure out how to trick it closed and keep it closed for as long as possible.

I tried the handle on the cage door of the storage locker. It was locked. I looked around for anything I could use to break in.

I grabbed a shovel and jammed the metal blade into the space between the panels. I had to lean to one side with all my might, but it worked. The lock snapped and the door swung open. I grabbed a helmet from the nearby lockers and put as many caps in it as I could fit. Then I gathered an armful of flares.

I dropped everything in a pile in front of the blast wall, then picked out one of detonator caps.

In case of an explosion or fire, the wall would crash

down. But there was a keypad on the core-scraper side that allowed someone to open the door once things were clear.

If they knew the code.

I didn't know the code, but someone else might, and I couldn't risk leaving it intact.

The pad was just above eye level and stuck out from the wall. I pushed the red ignition button on the det-onator and placed it on top of the keypad. I now had five minutes to get clear before the cap blew. At least I hoped I had five minutes. My dad had only ever showed me one of these caps in a safety manual. *In case you ever find yourself working in the mines*. He must have been clairvoyant.

I walked back underneath the jagged teeth of the blast door, searching the ceiling with my headlamp until I found what I was looking for, a small metal box about fifteen feet away from the opening. It was a smoke detector.

I arranged a bunch of uniforms in a pile right under-neath. It looked a little like a fire pit, the kind we'd make on camping trips back on Earth, which is exactly what I was going for.

Then I lit a flare. One wouldn't be enough, so I tossed it into the middle of the pit. Smoke began to rise. I lit another flare, and then another and another until the whole pile was in flames.

The smoke rose higher and higher, pooling around the sensor, getting thicker and darker.

Then the cloud began to descend, which was a bad thing for our lungs. If this plan didn't work, I'd have to put out the fire and then get the kids to run away as fast as we could, which I was willing to bet wasn't as fast as an armed shooter.

I could hear the others back down the tunnel starting to move, their helmet lights bobbing in the gathering haze. My father had said he was going to buy us time. I might need to do the same thing to give those kids a chance to escape.

I fumbled the remaining detonator caps between my fingers, ready to throw them into the fire if it came to that. The explosion might destroy this tunnel, taking me with it, but it would stop whoever was coming after us.

The elevator must have been descending by now.

Why wasn't the blast door closing? I fought a rising sense of panic.

I waved my arms to send more plumes toward the ceiling.

Then a light shone at my feet. It started as a sliver, then grew wider and wider.

The elevator had returned, and it was opening.

Just then the cap on the keypad exploded. The force of the blast knocked me to the ground.

I landed on my side. I flipped onto my stomach and prepared to jump up and fight, but before I could, the smoke detector finally kicked in.

The last thing I saw was a pair of black boots running toward me, and then the blast door slammed shut. The logo for Melming Mining glowed brilliantly in the light of the flares.

I quickly got back up and ran to the fire extinguishers. A wave of relief washed over me.

We were safe—for now. But whoever was on the other side knew there were survivors. The blast door would slow them, but if they wanted to come after us, I worried they'd find a way.

I doused the flames, then turned to run.

I realized with a sudden sense of dread that this was our life now. Every step we took would lead to one more decision, one more escape.

Every time we put out one fire, another would spring up.

There wasn't going to be an end, not until we found the beacon, and not until the end of the Blackout.

I hurried to join the others. I passed the infirmary.

Alek was still lying on the cot. Mandeep was shaking him to try to get him to move.

He didn't budge.

"Mandeep. Why aren't you moving?"

"Pavel said to leave Alek. He said he was going to slow us down. I can't leave him."

The lights ahead were still going up and down, illuminating the walls of the tunnel. The group wasn't moving nearly fast enough. I stepped into the infirmary and whispered to Mandeep.

"We need to run now and get far away fast."

She looked at Alek. "He's so weak. He needs our help."

"There are other kids out there who are going to need our help. Life down here is going to be dangerous. They're going to need your medical expertise."

"I can't leave him. He's sick," she said, her voice shaky.

I drew a deep breath and looked at my feet. Was that something I could do? Leave Alek behind?

Then I saw something I hadn't noticed before.

The cart Alek was lying on had wheels.

"Mandeep, help me unlock these. We'll roll him, or wheel him with us as fast as—"

"No," Alek said. The sound of his voice shocked me.

"Alek, we have to go!" Mandeep said.

He shook his head violently. "No."

I ignored him and reached down to unlock the wheels. His fist slammed into the back of my head, and I saw a yellow flash in front of my eyes. I braced myself for another blow, my head swimming.

"Alek! Stop!" Mandeep yelled. I heard his fist connect with Mandeep, and she fell back, sending a cart of medical tools skidding across the floor.

I got up and peered through the bursts of light. Alek was swinging wildly. I lunged at him, wrapping my arms around his chest.

"Alek, we're all dealing with stuff. But you need to come with us. We need to go now!"

He was much stronger than I expected, especially for someone who hadn't eaten in days. He flexed his arms, breaking my hold, then spun and swung at me. I ducked just in time, but I slipped and fell back.

Alek reached down. He grabbed a small hammer, like the kind doctors use to make your knee kick, and for a horrible instant I was sure he was going to attack me.

Instead he began pounding one of the wheels, bending the metal support until it was a twisted useless mess. Then he destroyed the others. Each time he thought we were coming to stop him, he would glare and swing the hammer in the air.

"No," he said, standing up. He threw the hammer away and then lay back on his cot, staring at the poster.

Mandeep's lips quivered. "Alek? We can't just leave you." She looked at me. "Christopher, we can't just leave him."

I took a deep breath. I took a step toward the cart, but Alek kicked out with his good leg, crunching my outstretched fingers.

"No," he murmured.

"Alek, there are people out in that tunnel who are your family now. We'll help you get through this."

I hoped the word *family* might tweak something, some kind of reaction. It didn't. He was as still as stone.

"Alek, please." I stepped toward him. He leaped from the cot, screaming and swinging wildly again. Mandeep and I retreated back through the door. Alek slammed it closed, then we heard him topple a large cabinet in front, jamming it shut.

I leaned my head on the door. I could hear Alek shuffling back to his cot.

"Alek."

He didn't answer.

I turned my head and stared at the blast door. Someone was on the other side. They'd come through eventually, and Alek would die if he were left here alone.

Maybe that was what he wanted? I pushed the infirmary door as hard as I could, but it wouldn't budge.

Mandeep put her hand to her mouth, tears welling in her eyes. She leaned against the wall of the tunnel.

"Alek," I said. "There's food in the fridge. There's water in the taps."

I debated my next words. It was a risky move, but I had to leave thinking there was at least a chance I wasn't condemning him to die alone.

"I know you'll want to follow us once you've had a chance to think about it. I'll make us easy to find. We'll go down Tunnel 3 and then take the third sub-entrance on the right. Then we will alternate left and right six times, that's three each, starting with a left turn. Remember the threes. You can find us."

Nothing.

I turned and took Mandeep's hand, and we ran to catch up to the others.

Chapter Ten
Chase

We caught up to the group quickly. Too quickly. We needed to move faster.

I sprinted ahead of them and waved for them to follow.

We made the first planned turn into the third shaft entrance on the right. This was a smaller tunnel, one of the exploratory holes that hadn't been fully dug out by an excavator yet.

A tall adult would probably bang his head on the ceiling, but we passed through easily. There were no emergency lights in these smaller holes, so we had to flick on our headlamps.

I looked back. Finn was bending down to hold Darcy's hand. He didn't look comfortable.

"I'm tired," I heard Darcy cry to Finn. "I need to stop."

I pulled to the side and leaned against the wall, waving for everyone to pass.

"Keep moving," I said. "Take the third turn on your left. Mandeep knows where to go from there."

Mandeep nodded as she passed.

Finn and Darcy caught up with me and stopped. Darcy sat on the floor, on the verge of tears, her eyes wide with terror.

Finn was puffing from the effort of pulling her along. "You rock, Finn, but I think you need a break."

Finn smiled. "Thanks, Chris." He turned to Darcy, "I'm going to run ahead. If you catch me, you can have my chocolate dessert!"

Darcy didn't move.

"I'm going," Finn said, turning and dramatically beginning to run. "Oh no, I better get going!" he said.

I leaned down to Darcy and said, "I'll carry you for a while. We can get him!"

I swung my pack around so it was on my chest, then I picked up Darcy and hoisted her onto my back. "Wrap your arms around my neck," I said. Then we started to run.

Finn gave a shriek of mock panic as we began to chase him, and Darcy actually giggled. I could have hugged Finn right then.

We alternated our path, Finn sometimes pretending to get tired and then sprinting again just as we approached him. Darcy even climbed down to run the last bit.

As we made our final turn, I could hear the sounds of the others up ahead. They'd reached the end of the twists and turns, and were collapsed in a semicircle on the floor, their headlamps glowing up and down the walls. They fought to catch their breath. Jimmi was lying down. He looked completely beat.

Darcy ran up to Finn and pretended she and Friendly were attacking him.

"Grrrr!" she growled.

Finn laughed as much as he could while he was winded, and fell to the floor, playing dead.

I leaned over, hands on my knees and fought the urge to throw up. I was covered in sweat. I checked my watch. The trip had taken us about half the day. Time-wise, we weren't very far from the entrance. But mathematically, I felt we were safe. I did a quick calculation of all the various other possible tunnel combinations. If someone were following us, they'd have to guess right at each step to find us.

Unless, of course, Alek told them the sequence. Why had he stayed?

Maria stood up. "I'm so hungry. Did anyone grab some extra snacks?"

"Did you?" Pavel asked.

"What's that supposed to mean?" Maria asked.

Pavel shrugged. "I'm not sharing my stash with anyone."

"What a jerk," Maria said.

"What did you call me?"

"What you are." Maria took a step toward Pavel, who stood up and looked ready to fight.

I hurried in between them and held my arms out.

"I know we're all on edge," I said. "And I know I was probably a little hyper about moving out so fast."

"No kidding," Pavel said.

"But fighting each other isn't going to solve anything. Let's just set up a new camp. We can figure out the food and water situation later. I still have some extra chocolate bars." I took a handful out of my backpack and tossed one to Maria and one to Pavel.

Pavel let his hit his chest and fall to the ground. He didn't take his eyes off Maria.

"First I want her to apologize," Pavel said through gritted teeth.

Maria took a bite of chocolate.

I looked at her, hoping my arched eyebrows would get across how important this was.

She lowered her hands. "Pavel, I'm sorry . . . sorry you're a selfish jerk!"

Pavel lunged. I pushed him back, but not before he took a swing that connected with my nose.

The blood seemed to shock Maria and Pavel back to their senses.

"I'm—I'm sorry, Christopher," Pavel sputtered. "It was an accident."

Maria also sounded contrite. "Yeah. Sorry. There's just, you know, a lot of stuff right now. . . ."

I nodded, holding my nose between my fingers. I pointed at Pavel, but I looked at Maria.

She lowered her head but said, "Sorry, Pavel."

He gave a quick nod, which I hoped was a sign of acceptance.

I moved away from the wall. The bleeding seemed to have stopped. "Okay, good. Just . . . let's all try to remember we have an enemy, and it's not anyone in this room."

They nodded.

Jimmi's headlamp scanned the tunnel. "Hey, where's Alek?"

Mandeep and I looked at each other. She gestured at me with her head.

"He locked himself in the infirmary," I said, giving the short version.

"He did what?" Jimmi and Pavel said together.

"I don't know. I have to hope he'll come to his

senses and follow us before he's in danger."

"How will he find us?" Jimmi asked.

"I told him the sequence of tunnels we'd be using. He can find us."

"What?" Pavel said. "What if he leads them right to us?"

"It was a risk," I said, "but a small one. Like I said, he'll come to his senses."

"Unless he's dead."

I nodded. "But that blast door is sealed shut. I'm hoping it can't be reopened."

"Then why did *we* run?" Maria said. It was a good question.

"Because there's a chance it will be reopened."

"Which brings us back to the stupidity of telling Alek how to find us!" Pavel said.

Everyone started arguing and talking over each other. I had just stopped one fight, and now it looked like everyone wanted a piece of me.

"Stop!" It was Finn. He was standing a few feet away, his fists at his side, his face pinched with anger. "Stop talking now!"

Everyone stopped.

Finn walked into the middle of the group. "Christopher has kept us safe and fed and made sure we had water ever since we came down here. How many of us thought to get Alek to the infirmary? How many of you have gone out looking for food and water for *everyone*, not just himself?" He looked pointedly at Pavel, who looked down at his feet. "How many of you stopped to help me and Darcy back in the tunnel?"

Suddenly everyone was looking at their feet.

"Exactly," Finn went on. "Does anyone else down here think they can do better?"

Nobody raised a hand. He gave a *humph* and then nodded at me.

"Thanks, Finn," I said. He nodded again and then walked back to help Darcy get a bed ready.

Pavel grabbed the chocolate bar I had thrown at him and stuffed it into his pocket.

I took all the food out my backpack and placed it on the floor.

"I'll go back and check on Alek soon if he doesn't find us first. But let's set up camp together. We can pool all our stuff right now and see what we have, okay?"

Jimmi nodded first. Maria was next, and then everyone joined me with the supplies from their packs.

Everyone had a helmet. Jimmi had even grabbed some extras to use once the batteries died. I kicked myself for not thinking of that, but I was glad somebody had.

"Nice work, Jimmi," I said, and meant it.

There was enough food and water for a few days if we rationed really well.

And, luckily, Pavel and Finn had grabbed a few extra coveralls, which meant we had something softer than rock to use as bedsheets and pillows.

Mandeep took a look at my nose and said it was probably *not* broken. It still throbbed like crazy, but I did my best not to show that.

I took first watch. I wasn't sleeping very much anyway, and volunteering was one more way I could show everyone I was willing to make sacrifices.

Snores filled the passageway. I found them kind of soothing. My dad snored so loud sometimes that he'd wake himself up. My mom used to joke that he peeled the paint off the walls, but for me, it was the sound of nighttime.

I walked a short way back up the tunnel, close enough to hear the sounds of sleeping kids, but far enough that I wouldn't bug anyone, and flicked on my headlamp.

I took out my copy of *Oliver Twist* and wrote the first variation of threes down on the back page. So the book was going to be a map after all, I thought.

Then I sat down and finally started to read Dickens's story.

The first chapter was all about a baby born in a

workhouse. There were a lot of long sentences that basically described him fighting for his first breath.

The baby was Oliver. The workhouse sounded like a horrible place, dingy and seedy.

I turned the page. His mom kissed him. Then she "shuddered; fell back—and died."

Died?

I snapped the book shut.

The image of my own mom's death floated in front of me.

I dug my fingernails into my palms to stop myself from crying out.

Now I knew what my dad meant when he told mom to read it to me when I was ready. No wonder that hadn't happened yet. This book was a one-way trip to misery town.

I took a deep breath and unclenched my fist. I stared at the red leather cover again.

I thought of the dedication inside. My own mother had never read it to me. I cracked the cover. I'd now read it for both of us, no matter how hard that would be.

This book meant something to my parents. You didn't give a random book about a mom dying in childbirth to someone who'd just given birth to a child.

Why was this book so special to them?

I started chapter two.

Chapter Eleven
Crumbs

I woke up with a shake, wiped my eyes, and ran my fingers over my face. Spit had dried all over my mouth. The tunnel was completely dark.

I flicked my headlamp. Nothing.

Stupid me. I'd fallen asleep reading the book, and my battery had run out.

Why had I wasted a precious source of light to read a book? That didn't make me a good leader. It made me an idiot.

Everyone else was still asleep, so I tiptoed back toward the camp, hoping I wouldn't trip over anyone or step on a sleeping head. As I got closer to the sound, I got on my hands and knees, feeling for a helmet.

Bingo. There was one just on the edge of the group.

I put my hand in front of the light to block it at least a bit and turned it on. It was Jimmi's. I tightened the strap and looked down at him, sleeping. There were crumbs around his mouth and an empty chocolate bar wrapper tucked into his hand.

He had taken them from the group pile. We were in danger of using up what little resources we had way too quickly, and Jimmi couldn't contain his sweet tooth? Anger flushed my cheeks. I had to talk to Jimmi, but that could wait. I remembered my own dead helmet light, another wasted resource, and felt ashamed but still angry. I walked over to the pile of extra helmets and grabbed one. I placed it next to Jimmi.

We needed to find more food. I knew there was still that break room in Tunnel 2, but that would only have snacks.

There had to be better-stocked refill stations somewhere else in the mines. These tunnels went on for miles and miles. Elena's father was always coming by to talk to my dad about working conditions. They'd describe the different shifts, and how the newer and longer tunnels took the workers farther away from the cafeteria for longer times.

They'd agreed on satellite break rooms, not with

fully equipped kitchens but with storage for small meals, snacks, and water. I knew the Tunnel 3 system was one of the longest, which was why I'd picked it for our escape. Lots of places to hide. We hadn't gone that far down the tunnel yet, but if we kept going, switching back to the main tunnel from time to time, we'd come on a break room eventually.

Jimmi had just volunteered to lead the first search.

I walked back to my book and my backpack, leaned against the wall, and flicked off my light. What else should we do next?

The last few days we'd done what my parents had said. We'd run. We'd hid. And we'd survived.

To keep doing that, I needed to explain to everyone what was going on, what we needed to do next, and why. I'd call a meeting before I sent Jimmi out.

And as I sat there in the dark, I began working on a speech.

It would need to be some kind of grand statement that would rally everyone to our goal: to find the beacon without a map and to somehow defeat the people who attacked us.

Who were they anyway? Why had they attacked us?

Were they pirates? Mercenaries? Attackers? Those

were kind of vague words. We needed something better to describe them.

As far as I knew, they weren't interested in the mines themselves. It had taken them three days to even come down to the basement. They were up top where they'd landed on Perses—landed and destroyed our lives.

Landers.

That was what I'd call them. That could also work as a kind of code word. Whenever anyone heard or said the word *Landers,* we'd know it was short for immediate danger, and we should run. It was way quicker than saying, *Those guys who attacked us up top and killed everyone* are back.

Landers it was.

Did that mean *we* also needed a name? I guess we did, something that sounded different from Landers.

I considered calling us Melmers, in honor of Hans Melming and his Great Mission. But as much as I admired Melming, that just sounded stupid.

What were we, orphans, like Oliver Twist? Yes. Olivers and Twisters sounded just as stupid as Melmers.

I couldn't believe I was wasting so much mental energy on this. Maybe I was avoiding the actual meat of the speech.

Tunnelers? If the Landers were on land, then we were

in the tunnels of the mine. Minors in the mine.

Wait, that was it. MiNRs. We were minors and we were miners.

When I spoke to everyone over breakfast and laid out my plan to keep moving and to survive, it would be the Landers against the MiNRs.

Now, what was I actually going to say?

Chapter Twelve

Speaking

"My mother said to me, before she was killed, that we needed to run. We have run. We have hid and we have survived. That's what we are going to keep doing! Together!"

I punched my fist in the air for emphasis.

My voice echoed off the empty tunnel walls.

I was convinced.

Now I just had to make the speech before an actual crowd of kids.

That was making me more nervous than I liked to admit. What if they mocked me? I remembered the first time I'd had to give an oral presentation in school. The topic was "The Great Mission for Kids." I'd prepared a whole mini-slide show about Melming, mining, space exploration, and how I was going to be the next great genius scientist.

A couple of kids had begun giggling when I'd said that last part. I was so rattled that I stumbled through the rest of my notes and lost my place. It was a mess.

Brock and Jimmi had made fun of me the entire recess.

"Hey, genius, maybe you can invent a machine to help you talk!"

"I love Melming so much. I want to kiss him. *Smooch smooch*."

Elena had defended me, but even she told me I had been "totally geeking out" and had needed to "dial it back" a bit.

Come to think of it, that was the first time Jimmi had called me Little Melming. I should have remembered it was an insult.

The next time I had to give a speech, I'd locked myself in the bathroom, my hands sweaty and cold. My mom had eventually lured me out and forced me to do the talk, but I'd just stared down at my notes and mumbled. *But that was then*, I told myself. *Suck it up*.

I had planned to give my speech after breakfast, but I'd panicked. Instead I sent Jimmi and Maria on the food search first.

They'd be back soon. I had to have something ready, so I went on a long walk to be alone and think. I continued my pattern of alternating left and right, rehearsing the speech where no one could hear me.

I knew I could find my way back quickly, so I wasn't really paying attention when I turned a corner and the light from my headlamp glinted off something shiny. I just kept practicing.

"My mother said to me. My mom's last words were. My mom, before she was killed by the Landers, turned to me." I practiced the inflections that would work best. Reading *Twist*, oddly, was helping me. Oliver's life was pretty horrible: getting accused of stealing and getting chased out of the orphanage. But he went on. I would go on. Maybe I should quote the book in my speech?

Distracted, I walked straight into something hard, smashing my knee. I tried to keep my balance while hopping on one foot. I failed and fell, banging my head hard on the ground. The impact tore my helmet loose, and it flew away. The headlamp shattered against the wall.

I was doubled over in pain, clutching my knee, and now I was without a light. Thankfully, my knee wasn't broken—just dinged—but it hurt.

What had I walked into?

I reached out slowly, and my fingers touched

something cool and metallic. That was unexpected.

Had I found one of the emergency batteries? If so, I'd better be careful touching more parts of it.

Was it another series of lockers? Was this one of the satellite break rooms?

I carefully ran my fingers along the smooth metal, then all of a sudden it wasn't so smooth. There was a discernable groove that ran diagonally as the metal began to slope downward.

A thrill was starting to climb up my spine. If this was what I hoped it was, this changed everything.

I let my fingers follow the slope until, *yes!* It ended in a very rough, almost thorny, cone about the size and shape of a spiky pineapple.

My heart raced, and a huge grin broke across my face.

I had stumbled on a digger, the undisputed technical marvel of the Melming Mining Company.

I'd read about them as a kid and had asked my dad to show me one on my first-ever trip to the mines on Perses. He'd snuck me into the garage. "But don't tell anyone. These babies are special." He'd tapped the side of one with his palm, eliciting a beautiful deep metallic sound.

"A digger is a one-person drilling machine. It can cut through rock like a knife through butter."

I had just stared in awe. It had looked like someone had glued a giant drill bit onto the front of a luxury sports car.

He'd pointed at the bit. "The whole front assembly is the borer. The spiky cone at the front is the key. It's called the disrupter. It's a mini-fusion reactor, and I don't totally get how it works."

I had almost automatically picked up where he'd left off. "It's called that because it uses a kind of energy field to 'disrupt' the matter in front of it." I had known I'd been geeking out a bit, as usual, but my dad had beamed.

"That's what they say. I do know that it lets the digger move at an incredible speed underground."

"It actually breaks apart the molecules, so it's like there's almost no resistance. It even pulls the digger forward faster."

He'd nodded. "But that also makes it really dangerous."

"How?"

"Well, the disrupter is, as you've pointed out, ripping matter apart. It's fine to do that when the reaction is contained by solid rock. But if you hit an air pocket, like a tunnel, the front can ignite all the oxygen and basically turn the air itself into a fire bomb."

"But that must happen all the time."

"It could. But the other little bit of genius is that the digger cone has a sensor. If it detects an air pocket, it shuts off immediately. Of course, that also means the digger is instantly reduced to a glorified golf cart. It doesn't move very fast at all when it's just running on its tracks."

"So how do you keep that from happening?"

"We put warning signals inside any big seams of air, tunnels, or big gaps in volcanic rock to warn the driver to stay clear."

His next words to me then were why everything had changed now.

"Would you like to take one for a spin?"

I knew how to drive one.

He'd made me promise never to tell anyone, but he'd sat me down on the seat next to him and we'd taken a joyride through solid rock. If his bosses had caught us, he could have been fired and sent back to Earth. But he'd said it was something I needed to know, and to heck with the rules.

He'd laughed as I'd fought the steering wheel and strained to reach the power pedals.

That was one of my favorite memories of him.

And it might be what saved us now.

I felt for a latch and opened the cockpit. The light inside came on immediately, so bright, I was almost blinded. Once my eyes adjusted, I could see that the machine in front of me was just one digger in a whole row of diggers.

I'd stumbled on a garage.

I quickly slid my way onto the seat and pushed the ignition button.

The digger fired up.

"Thanks, Dad," I whispered as I began to maneuver the gears.

I was no expert, and it took me about five minutes to turn the digger around so I could drive into the tunnel nose first. I pushed another button, and a guide light shone out from the cone.

I was about to turn left, to head back to the camp, when I thought of Alek. I also thought of the food and water we'd left behind.

I turned right, toward the infirmary, advancing slowly, staying as close to the wall as I could.

In a pinch I could dig straight into the rock, but I knew my way back better through the tunnels. Finally I arrived at the infirmary door. I pulled even with it and turned off the digger.

I hit the release button, and the hatch opened slowly. I was careful to turn off the light first. I listened. There was no noise at all other than the cooling engine.

"Alek," I whispered. "Alek, it's me, Christopher. I'm back. I came back."

Silence.

I pushed the door, and to my surprise it swung open easily. Alek's helmet was still hanging on the hook by the door.

This was not a good sign.

I put it on, switched on the light, and scanned the room.

All the cots were empty.

Alek was gone.

The poster he'd been staring at for days was gone.

I searched for any clues of what had happened: missing sheets, pillows, missing medical supplies. Everything seemed the same as we'd left it. I got down on all fours and searched for dirt, footsteps in the dust, or possibly even blood.

Nothing.

My heart raced. Had he tried to follow us? Surely, I'd have seen him on my drive back. If he had followed us, why hadn't he taken the helmet?

Had he been taken?

I turned off the lamp and crept back out of the infirmary, my ears and eyes on high alert. I slunk into the cockpit of the digger and started it up.

As I inched forward, the blast door came into view.

It was open.

The Landers were in the tunnels.

I slammed the digger into reverse, crunching into the wall as I turned. I had to get back to the camp the fastest way possible, and that was a straight line.

I flicked open the red safety cap and activated the disrupter. Immediately the cone began to spin. I angled the digger toward the nearest wall and floored the speed pedal. My father had handled this on our joyride. I hoped I'd done everything right.

The digger sped forward. I closed my eyes, half expecting to smash like a tin can against the hard rock wall. But then, without even noticing the moment, I was inside solid rock. I opened my eyes. Sparks and flashes illuminated the window.

It was like being inside the northern lights. It was beautiful.

The compass on the dashboard pointed almost straight ahead. I was pretty sure I was heading in the right direction to hit the camp. At the speed I was traveling, I calculated that it should only take me a minute.

The digger began to beep, and I looked with a panic at the screen. A red light was flashing on the map, straight ahead.

An air pocket. The tunnel!

I veered to the right. The digger responded, easily turning at top speed, but I needed to slow down. The last thing I wanted to do was land in the middle of the kids I was trying to save with a red-hot digger.

The digger blasted through the wall and landed with a thud on the floor.

The sensor kicked in, instantly stopping the disrupter. My head snapped back, and it took me a second to realize what I was seeing.

All the lights were on, the real lights, and the tunnel was completely illuminated.

A mostly bald figure in combat pants and a leather jacket was facing all the kids, who were backing up against the wall.

I was too late.

The Landers had reached the camp ahead of me.

I jumped out of the digger, shouting, ready to attack with my fists, helmet—whatever I could grab. "Get away from those kids, Lander!"

The figure turned around.

I stopped. I hadn't been shot, but I felt like I had.

Elena Rosales grinned at me and scoffed. "What the heck is a Lander?"

Chapter Thirteen
Sleepwalking

I sat against the side of the tunnel with my knees scrunched up between my arms, keeping my distance from Elena, who was sitting with her back against the opposite wall, her legs stretched out in front of her. She couldn't seem to keep them still.

We were able to turn off the lights in one section of the tunnel, so that became the sleeping quarters. Everyone else had gone to bed, but Elena and I moved back to a lighted part to talk.

She was filling me in on what had happened since the attack, but I just stared at her, dumbstruck.

I remembered the feel of her fingertips on mine just before the bombs hit. Her lips were moving, but I could only remember how close they'd been to mine just before the Landers had attacked.

It had been only three days, but she was so different in every possible way. She had shaved half of her head.

"Most of it had burned off in the attack. I just finished it off," she said. "I'm not sure how much will grow back, if any."

There were wounds on her face.

"When the bullets started flying, I was hit, more by the shrapnel than the bullets."

"So you were able to get up after that first bomb hit us?"

She nodded. "I was on the playground when another bomb went off. I woke up covered in rubble. By some miracle, the metal from the swing set had created a kind of roof over me. I was pinned, but not crushed. I could breathe, and I could see. I could also hear that the shooting had ended. I stayed as still as possible until I saw a chance to escape."

"Escape?"

"It wasn't really an escape in the end. They kind of all left, and I got up and made my way down here. I'd seen your dad grab you and head for the roof, so I figured that's where everyone went—everyone who wasn't killed."

I swallowed the lump in my throat. "Did you see him die?"

Elena shook her head. "They'd all retreated to the middle of the field, trying to draw the fire away from the core-scraper. I was running to help them, or die with them, when the second bomb knocked me out."

We were silent for a long time. I stared at Elena while she rubbed her legs and stared at the ground.

She lifted her head and looked straight into my eyes. "Then, after they—what did you want us to call them, oh, Fearless Leader? Landers?"

I nodded.

She rolled her eyes. "After the *Landers* left, I snuck back into the core-scraper through a crack in the roof. There were plenty of those. I grabbed some supplies from my apartment, changed, and hailed the elevator. To be honest, I was totally surprised that the elevator worked."

"So was I. If I'd known it was you—"

"It took me a whole day to figure out a way to open that stupid blast door by the way. Thanks for shutting that on me."

"I'm sorry. . . ."

Elena held up her hand. "I'm just hassling. It was a sound decision. Real leadership, in fact." She actually gave me a little salute that didn't seem ironic.

"I saw black boots under the door. You were wearing red boots at the party."

"They were red," she said, lifting her leg so I could get a closer look. The boots had been scorched black, the leather cracking and flaking. Elena's pants rode up her leg a bit, and I could see blisters and burns on her as well. She quickly tugged her pant leg into her socks.

"Are you okay?" I asked, shaken.

"Sure." She shrugged. "I basically had to rip the leggings off. They'd melted into my skin, so some of the skin came off too."

"That . . . sucks."

She shrugged. "Yeah. But I'm alive. Once I was in the infirmary, I was able to put some cream on the worst burns. My legs feel better now, more irritated than painful."

The infirmary. I'd forgotten all about Alek!

"Did you see Alek?"

"I saw him. He's alive."

I let out a relieved whew.

"I should say he was barely alive, more like a zombie. As soon as I came through the infirmary door, he came rushing at me with a scalpel. Luckily, I recognized him and yelled, 'Alek, it's me, Elena!' One look at me and he just dropped the scalpel and stood there like a statue."

"So why isn't he with you?"

"He followed me for a bit while I walked around looking for a way to turn off those stupid emergency flashers and get some real light down here."

"The emergency backup room? I looked for it."

"It's just past the entrance to Tunnel Four, but you probably didn't know that. Alek started muttering something about threes and rights and lefts, and then he just sat down on the floor and refused to move."

"I gave him directions to follow us."

"I figured that out pretty quickly, but he'd forgotten the first bit." Elena stared at me. "But I know how your brain works, Christopher Nichols, and figured if you ended with three you'd start with three, so I headed down Tunnel Three."

"That's how you found the camp."

She nodded. "It took a while for the lights to actually kick in, which is why the kids looked so scared when I showed up, and then you blasted out of the wall like that. I guess there are no adults down here?"

I shook my head.

"Didn't think so." She stared at the floor again.

"But Alek is still out there," I said. "We have to go find him."

Elena didn't move. "I couldn't carry him in the dark. He was asleep when I left, hugging some crumpled-up piece of paper. I'm sure we can find him in the morning."

I calmed down, but my head was still swimming with questions.

"Wait, how did you open the blast door again?"

"My dad was the foreman down here, remember? I knew there was always a backup system, even for the backup systems."

"Meaning?"

"Meaning that your detonator cap only blew off the top layer of the panel. The wires underneath were still there. I just needed to figure out a way to get them to recognize the right sequence of electronic bursts. I tapped them together in different combinations, and one of them finally worked."

I must have looked skeptical.

"What, you think you're the only genius here?" She smiled, a real smile, and for a moment I saw the old Elena.

I smiled too.

"I looked for you right after the first bombs hit," I said.

She closed her eyes. The smile vanished.

Idiot, I said to myself.

"It was chaos up there. I was in a crater after the first bomb, then running through that black smoke, then under that pile of rubble. There was probably no way you'd have seen me. The Landers didn't, thank goodness." She paused and gave a deep sigh. "They just marched straight at the field, firing at everything that moved, or didn't."

"I saw it too."

She paused. "You saw some. After you left." It almost sounded like an accusation. "After you left, I heard them talking. They walked all around me, giving orders. Some spoke English. Some spoke Spanish. Some spoke other languages I couldn't pick up. They'd been waiting for the Blackout. They are here to steal the ore."

"Any idea who they're working for?"

She shook her head. "Once they finished attacking, they all got back in the ship and just took off."

"Which direction?"

"South."

I nodded. "Toward the main storage depots."

"Duh. They're pirates, Christopher. They'll take everything and leave us here to die."

"So they don't even know there are survivors down here?"

Elena gave an annoyed snort. "Either they didn't see

or they didn't care. What can a bunch of kids do, right?" Something in her tone suggested she agreed.

"Even if they do know about us, they probably just figure we'll die of starvation."

"They might be right," Elena said. "I saw what you left behind in the cafeteria. There's not enough food there to last more than a month."

"We'll find more."

Elena smirked. "The break rooms? There's not enough in those, either. Where do you think all the extra food for the party came from? And how long do you think all those vegetables and stuff will last before they go bad, even in a refrigerator?"

I had actually thought of that, but it was not a cheery thought, so I changed the subject.

"Just one ship?

Elena threw up her hands. "Yes. One ship. One *big* ship. One big enough to carry them and their weapons."

"So they all left," I said, thinking out loud. "Which means we can go back into the core-scraper for more salvage to help us survive."

She stood up suddenly and glared at me. Her voice was trembling.

"Survival? That's your big plan?"

"Survive. That's what we do. What we need to—"

She cut me off. Her eyes were blazing. "We need to fight! That's what you should be working out. A battle plan. How do we fight those stupid Landers? How do we kill them?" Elena was now standing over me, her fists clenched so tightly, her fingers were turning white.

Her rage took me off guard. I stayed on the floor and looked straight ahead, avoiding her eyes.

"We can't fight them."

"Christopher. They killed our parents. They killed our friends. They killed children."

I said nothing.

"We have to fight!"

I tried to sound as calm as possible. "We are kids, not soldiers. Fighting the Landers will guarantee we all die."

"This is a war." She punctuated each word with a poke of her finger.

I shook my head. "No. It's not. What we have here now is a different kind of mission."

She snorted. "You really are the same kid. The Great Mission and all that garbage. How's that working out for us?"

I ignored the jab. "My father made me promise that I'd protect them. He made me promise to be a leader."

"You want to be a leader? Give those kids something to fight for."

Now my anger rose, and I glared at her. "I *am* a leader. A 'fearless leader,' as you keep telling me, and I have kept these kids, *kids*, safe for a whole week. We have diggers. We can use them to move around, stay away from the Landers. We can find food, we can survive. We are still alive and we have a goal."

She shook, her jaw clenched, her hands in tight fists. Just a few days ago we'd stood even closer, and she'd almost kissed me. Now she looked like she wanted to kill me.

"What goal? To sit here and wait for the Landers to actually come through that blast door? For the Landers to leave? To die in some stupid cave-in, or die after they leave, waiting for somebody to come save us? Earth has no idea what's happened up here."

"We can let them know," I said quietly.

"How?"

"There's a beacon." I lifted my head and stared straight at her. She didn't seem as impressed as I'd hoped.

"A what now?" she said, cocking her head.

"A beacon. My dad told me there's a warning beacon that can send a message back to Earth."

"So, where is it? Did he leave directions? A map?"

"Not exactly."

"Not exactly?"

"I think I had a map, but I lost it."

"You think?"

I nodded.

"I think your dad made it up to get you in the elevator and give you some bizarre sense of hope."

I thought of how my father had stared at me when he'd given me the backpack and the book. He hadn't been lying. "It's real," I said firmly.

She lifted and dropped her arms in frustration. "It doesn't even matter."

"Why not?"

"Your plan is to get all these kids searching a giant underground maze for weeks, with no supply of food and water, for something completely hidden and completely useless."

"We can use it to signal Earth."

Elena scoffed. "There's a blackout, remember?"

"After the Blackout ends."

"We'll all be *dead*!" she yelled. The sound echoed off the tunnel walls.

"Shhhhh. Keep your voice down. I already told you we can find more food and water. We can survive."

Elena paced the floor. When she finally spoke again, she almost hissed. "You know how I said they were walking all around me as I lay there, burned, *alone*, and covered in junk? They weren't doing their morning exercise. They were laying bombs to destroy everything, including the terra-forming equipment and the water reservoirs. Once they are gone, the Perses colony will be nothing more than rubble and corpses."

She let that sink in.

I knew right away what she meant. The Landers wouldn't destroy the terra-forming technology until they were safely off the planet. They needed it too.

They'd wait until they were done, they'd leave, and then they'd trigger the bombs. If they'd done it right, it would look like there'd been some accident during the Blackout.

News would never reach Earth about anything if those bombs were detonated.

The Landers would get away with no witnesses and no evidence they'd ever been here. The beacon would never be activated.

The Blackout would get the blame.

Elena took a step toward me. "Not doing anything to stop them is suicide. And running is not doing anything. We will have to fight. Are you a leader who can help us do that?"

I was shaking, but Elena was right. The Landers were true enemies, and I couldn't make her an enemy as well.

"I don't want to fight you, Elena." I paused and sighed. "And you *are* right. We will need to fight the Landers."

She softened her stance.

"But doing it now would also be suicide." I paused again, trying to search her face for some sign of my friend. "We can train the older kids—Pavel, Jimmi, and Maria—to drive, fight. We can strategize. I can't do it alone."

"Meaning?"

"Elena, I need your help."

A glimmer of the Elena I knew crept back into her eyes.

She gave an almost imperceptible nod. Then she saluted and turned and walked silently back to the camp.

Chapter Fourteen
Drive Shaft

Elena told me where to look for Alek. I fired up the digger and found him sleeping exactly where she'd described. He hadn't moved an inch.

Alek was pale and cold, and looked like a ghost. I tried to grab the crumpled Melming Mining poster from his hands, but he clutched it so tightly, it began to rip, so I stopped.

But there was hope. He had gotten up and tried to find us. He wasn't trying to fight me anymore. I maneuvered him into the cockpit seat and crammed in beside him. I turned on the digger, and we drove back to camp.

He still wasn't talking, other than some indecipherable mumbles. The only words I could pick up were *three* and *Rosales*. He might have said *Brock*, but he dozed off.

Back at camp I lifted him out of the cockpit and laid him on a makeshift cot Mandeep had set up with some blankets and coveralls. He woke up and gave a start upon seeing Elena again.

Elena somehow managed to get him to eat sliced celery and drink chocolate milk. He threw up the first few mouthfuls, but he finally kept some down. The color started to come back in his cheeks, and he even nodded a thanks to Elena and Mandeep.

I watched Elena, impressed with how she was able to work with him. She relaxed when she spoke, coaxing him to eat. Or maybe she was just trying to get one more soldier healthy and ready for the coming fight?

Later that evening I read a few more chapters of *Oliver Twist*. Maybe I'd been hoping to find the map, to prove to Elena that the beacon was real. But there was no map—just the continuing saga of Oliver the orphan.

Oliver grew up, escaped the orphanage, and became part of a band of street kids, being trained as a thief and a pickpocket by an old man named Fagin. Oliver was befriended by another orphan, the Artful Dodger, who was funny and incredibly skilled at lifting the valuables out of the coats of passing pedestrians. They'd walk away with no clue they'd just been robbed.

The Dodger got me thinking.

"Time to meet, Fearless Leader," Elena said, interrupting my thoughts. "I'll go get everyone together so you can rally the troops."

I nodded, shaking my head at her use of the word *troops*. I watched her walk away, took a deep breath, and braced myself for my speech. Elena's return had delayed it, but it was now time to put my nerves aside. The sound of approaching footsteps still made my pulse race.

Finn was putting Darcy to bed while the rest of us gathered around the digger.

I leaned against it and began to speak.

"We need to talk together about what to do.

"Food needs to be rationed. I know some of you have been tempted to sneak some extras"—I tried not to look at Jimmi—"and that's okay, but it has to stop now.

"We need to conserve water.

"We need to find toilet paper.

"We need to *not fight* each other." I rubbed my nose and glanced at Pavel, his mouth set in a thin line.

"We have to keep moving." With this last one, I rapped my knuckles on the digger for effect, and smiled. "And all the things I just mentioned get a lot easier with this."

Elena jumped in before I could go on. "There are more than a dozen diggers. We can use them to run, hide, look for food, explore, survive. But . . . we can also use them to fight."

That made me flinch. I didn't want Elena to mention that possibility yet. It was too scary a thought, and I could see everyone start fidgeting—stealing glances at each other. Maria began shaking.

I quickly stepped in front of Elena and held my hands up to calm everyone. "Not that we are going to do that unless we absolutely have to, and I don't see that happening anytime soon. Our job now is to stay safe and alive."

Elena began shuffling a pebble on the ground with her foot, refusing to look up at me.

"The diggers can help us move, find food and water, and I know how to drive one. But we can all learn how. And there's no time like the present."

To show how easy it was to drive one, I jumped into the cockpit of my digger and fired it up, moving slowly down the tunnel.

I looked back, expecting to see a MiNR parade, but only Elena was following. I turned off the engine and stood up.

"What's going on?" I asked. "It's not far, and we can all drive back."

Maria and Mandeep walked away from us. Maria cried, "I'm not ready. I can't."

Mandeep draped her arm around Maria's shoulders and led her back to the beds.

I looked at Elena, who was frowning at them.

Jimmi stood with his arms crossed, sneering at the digger. "Only an idiot would get behind the wheel of that deathtrap. I'm no idiot. You wanna kill yourself, Little Melming, go right ahead."

Pavel pressed his lips even more tightly together and did not say a word.

"I'll go!" someone called, running up to the digger. Finn. "This looks *so cool*! You'd have to be an idiot *not* to want to drive one." He leaned his head into the cockpit and looked at the glowing panel, letting out a low whistle. "Awesome."

Elena looked at him quizzically but smiled. "That's the spirit," she said.

His enthusiasm didn't work on Maria's sadness, but it did seem to dig at Jimmi's and Pavel's pride.

Pavel took a step toward us and then looked at Jimmi. "Whatsa matter, Murphy? Scared?"

Jimmi gritted his teeth. "Scared that a moron like you

will crash into me." But he started following as well. Before anyone could change their minds, I sat back down and drove to the garage.

The practice sessions continued for a few days. Finn was a natural, as was Elena. Jimmi was getting the knack of it, but Pavel was going to need more practice—he was always forgetting to start his disrupter before hitting the wall.

Mandeep was able to coax Maria into taking part, as long as Maria was guaranteed she wouldn't have to fight. We combined the driving lessons with work, driving from camp to the infirmary and cafeteria, grabbing as many supplies as we could. We also grabbed the mattresses off the cots.

I'd stayed behind on the last of these trips to take one final search of the elevator shaft, hoping to find some trace of the lost map. I tried digging into the debris but found nothing. I did find out that all the elevator shafts had now been filled with fallen rock and concrete, so there was no way left for us to go up, or for anyone else to come down.

I drove back, both sad and cheered by the thought.

Elena was waiting for me by the other diggers.

"I think we need to have a real training exercise," she

said before I could even get out of my cockpit.

"I've been thinking the same thing."

She nodded. "Good. A mock attack then?"

I sighed. "Elena, you saw the reaction when you even suggested the thought of a fight. These guys are not ready yet."

"You know we have to fight, and soon."

I hung my head. "Elena, why are you so eager to risk everyone's lives?"

"Christopher, do you know what a real leader has to do in a real war?"

"This isn't a real war."

She ignored that. "Coventry," she said. "That's how far a real leader is prepared to go."

"I don't even know what that means."

"It was during World War Two. The English had cracked a German code. They could track all the German troop movements, ships, planes, submarines. It could turn the tide of World War Two. One of the first things they deciphered was a German plan to bomb a city, Coventry."

I stared at her, unsure where she was going.

"You want to be a leader? Okay, imagine you're the top guy in England. You just found out Germany is going to bomb Coventry. What do you do?"

"Save Coventry?"

"If you save Coventry, it tips off the Germans that you know the code, and they'll never use it again."

"So what did he do?'

"He let the Germans bomb Coventry. At least, that's the story."

I paused. "That's horrible."

"No. That's how far a true leader has to go. In war, you sometimes have to sacrifice your own people to win."

I thought about what she was saying. Could I ever do that? No. And I hoped I never had to truly find out.

"How about a different kind of story?" I said at last, thinking of the Artful Dodger. "Pickpockets."

She stared at me. "Is this a joke?"

"No. It's from a book. If you are smaller and unarmed, you can't fight back on equal terms. Instead you take what you can when you can."

She cocked her head. "I'm listening," she said.

"We are not ready for a fight, *but* . . . small targeted raids could work. Raids designed to slow the Landers down, frustrate their efforts, and keep them here longer, ideally, until the Blackout is over and we can alert Earth. And if we can do those raids quickly and stealthily, we can get away alive."

"Guerilla tactics?" Elena said, nodding, but clearly still debating. "Could work. But we have to strike fast. What should we target?"

I pulled out my notebook. "The storage depots. I've done some calculations about how much ore has been mined since we arrived on Perses. The ship you saw is clearly meant to haul cargo."

"They certainly cleared more storage space by dropping hundreds of bombs."

"And much of the ore that's been moved from here to the main depot hasn't been processed."

"They still need to separate the actual minerals from the rock."

I nodded. "Again, I'm just going by some rough estimates, but I think it will take them the better part of the Blackout to do that."

"And once they are done, they'll go back to Earth, and we'll die a fast or a slow death up here on Perses."

"And they've already been on Perses for more than a week."

"Well, Fearless Leader, let's get everyone ready."

Chapter Fifteen
Disasters

The first raid was my idea, and it was a disaster.

It wasn't even a real raid. We staged a mock attack on the core-scraper, just to see how well we could get in, get out, and use the diggers to maneuver in the rock.

We lost our first digger when Mandeep swerved too quickly and ripped into the engine block of Finn's machine. It could have been way worse. A foot closer to the cockpit, and Finn would have been seriously injured or killed.

After extracting Finn from the wreckage, we reassembled outside the infirmary.

"Look, everyone. You've got to pay closer attention to the directional indicator on the map. The arrow needs to be pointing directly ahead, right up the middle. If it swerves, it means you are off course." We'd gone through this in training over and over, but in the stress of a real, or close to real, scenario, it had been one of the first lessons they'd forgotten.

Elena stood next to me. "There's also a motion sensor on the front of the digger. It picks up vibrations in the rock. It will alert you if you are close to something that's moving."

"So you can avoid loose rock or other diggers."

Mandeep's shoulders sagged. I wasn't trying to make her feel bad, but we couldn't afford to mess up in a real raid.

"It's a lot to keep track of, I know. That's why today is just a practice run."

Elena stood with her arms behind her back and began to pace from side to side. "MiNRs, listen up. We want to attack in a line, left to right. But we don't want them to anticipate where we're coming from. So we also want to stagger the ETA of our entry into the target."

"Can you put that in English, General Rosales?" Jimmi said.

Elena scowled as Pavel joined in. "Shall we recon with a mission over and out, and rejig with a . . . ," he said, smirking.

I frowned at both of them. "The idea is to have one of us do quick salvage while the others are there for backup."

"Or demolition," Elena added. "Don't worry too much about destroying stuff. You have to break a few eggs to make an omelet."

"The main thing is to get in and out quickly. This is a mock raid, not a mock battle." I stole a quick glance at Elena. She was frowning. "And remember that we can talk at close range," I added. "The diggers have radio capability."

Elena pointed toward the ceiling. "The Landers can't pick up the signal way up there. Things will be a bit different for a real raid when we're closer to them."

"But for today feel free to keep your radio on for the whole drill."

"Otherwise, pretend this is a raid on a Lander food depot. Don't worry about taking prisoners," Elena said, a steely look in her eyes. I felt a pang of sadness. As much as Elena had agreed to my plan for mini-raids, I knew that she really wanted to fight, and kill, Landers. All I could do was hope that never had to happen.

I strapped on my helmet. "Let's get back in those diggers. Aim for the twenty-eighth floor. We cut in from the exterior wall. In and out quickly." I had a faint hope we might find the lost map on the twenty-eighth floor. I was tempted to tell everyone else about the map and the beacon, but I remembered the blasting Elena had given me, so I kept it quiet for now.

"Let's see what we're capable of," Elena said.

We fired up the diggers and cut into the rock, rising toward the ruined hull of the core-scraper on a steep angle.

We reached the level of the twenty-eighth floor, then flattened out and approached in a set sequence. I went first, Pavel second, then Mandeep and Finn. Elena would come at the floor last, "sneaking in" as the imaginary "Landers" were distracted. She would steal some food or sabotage some part of their operation.

Pavel swerved unexpectedly before we'd gone more than a few feet, gunning his engine and cutting right across my path. My disrupter hit the resulting air pocket and stalled. I was supposed to be the first one into the building, but now I'd be lucky if I got there before Elena. That was worse than not getting there at all, at least for the sake of our little rehearsal.

"I'm out," I called into the radio. "Number One is down."

"Wimp," Elena called back.

"Ha-ha," I said, but I smiled. Joking was one way to

alleviate the stress. . . . That was, if she were joking.

"I'm going in," Mandeep called over the radio. I heard the sound of cracking concrete, then a much louder rumble. "Uh, guys. I think I just took out a support beam." As if to back her up, the rumble got louder.

"That was Finn," Mandeep said. "He just took out another beam. Stuff falling all over the place!" She sounded panicked.

The rumble grew even louder, and constant.

This was a very bad thing.

The core-scraper wasn't as stable as I'd hoped. The top floors must have continued to collapse. The pillars had been holding it up.

"Elena, pull back! Abandon!" Mandeep called into her radio. Then her radio went silent.

"Negative," Elena said. "I'm going in. I need to test my aim."

"Get out of there!" I yelled. "Everyone back to the camp. Now!"

"I can't see Mandeep anymore," Finn said, his voice trembling.

"Finn! Reverse, reverse!" I yelled. I could hear him through his radio firing up his engine and slamming it into reverse.

I hoped my disrupter had cooled enough to start up.

I nudged against the wall and fired it up. It burned blue and began dismantling the rock. I gunned the engine and sped toward the core-scraper.

I broke through the wall close to Mandeep. Her digger was crushed, a giant slab of concrete pinned down the entire front section.

I slammed my fist against my steering wheel.

Then I saw something moving in the cockpit. She was alive!

I turned my digger toward her. My disrupter had shut off, but the drill would work. I cut through the debris between us slowly. I could see her fingers scraping against the latch, desperately trying to escape before more concrete came crashing down.

"I'm almost there. Hold on!" I yelled, though I suspected she couldn't hear me.

I began digging through the slab that was pinning the cockpit lid down. The drill ate away, sending chunks of the concrete flying.

Just then Elena shot through right next to me. Her aim was accurate but incredibly ill-timed. She slammed sideways into my rear, knocking me off target.

The front of my digger listed to the left and began slicing into the shell of Mandeep's cockpit. A few more seconds and she would be shredded. I strained with all my might to turn the steering wheel back to the right. I could feel the muscles in my arm ready to rip. With a lurch, the digger moved and began slicing back into the concrete. Finally the slab spit apart completely. Mandeep shoved her latch open and flew out of the wreckage.

I opened my cockpit and pulled her in next to me. I closed the lid.

"Hold on," I said.

Mandeep was breathing so fast, I thought she might explode. I slammed the digger in reverse, swung to face the rock, and ignited my disrupter.

We sped back to camp.

Mandeep practically leaped from the cockpit, stumbled to her bed, and curled up in a ball under her sheets.

Maria marched up to me angrily. "What did you do?" she spit an inch from my face.

"There was a problem with the structure of the floor. I got her out. She'll be okay."

"She better be," Maria said, shoving me backward. Then she sat down next to Mandeep and patted her hand, whispering to her softly. Soon they were both asleep.

I knew how she felt.

Why hadn't Elena listened to me? Why hadn't she stopped?

She'd always been like that, of course. *A force of nature* is what my mom used to call her.

But putting everyone else at risk? That wasn't the Elena I knew.

I knew I wasn't the same Christopher. But I held out hope that if we could just get through this, get through the horror, then we'd be friends again. Maybe we'd be more than that.

I was lost in these thoughts when Elena returned. She leaped out of her cockpit with a huge smile.

"That was a blast!" she said, slapping me on the shoulder. "I can't wait to do it for real!"

"You could have gotten us all killed!" I hissed, trying not to wake Mandeep.

Elena took a step back. Her smile evaporated, and her face was as still as stone. "This isn't a game, Nichols. We need to know what we're capable of."

"I know. You said that. Well, one of the things you need to 'be capable of,' *Rosales*, is following the plan. Or would you prefer to spend our first real raid back here, babysitting?" I thought sounding like Elena might get her to listen to me.

Elena glared at me. I couldn't tell if she was hurt or just angry.

"Remember when we all agreed we needed to work

together? We still need someone to act as a leader, and that seems to be my job, so let me lead. That means that when I say get out, you get out. Do. You. Understand?"

She continued to glare, saying nothing. She swung her backpack off her shoulder and opened it up. It was filled with food and supplies she'd salvaged from the core-scraper.

I stared, incredulous.

"How?" I said, not quite able to visualize how she could have done all this in just a few minutes in the middle of a collapsing building. "That's amazing," I said.

"Not questioning your authority, sir." She stood back up straight. "I hit your digger, but if you'd operated according to plan or signaled your location over the radio, I could have avoided you. I knew I was supposed to arrive close to Mandeep, so I was planning on saving her. When I saw you were there, I decided to actually test our original plan and do a search for supplies. I found some."

I started to feel guilty about ripping into her, even though she had disobeyed an order. "You could have told me your plans too."

Elena gave a quick nod. "Noted. Communication will be more open in future, sir."

"Don't use the military lingo."

Elena paused and in barely a whisper said, "It helps . . . me." There was something in her voice, a slight tremor. She even bit her bottom lip. Everyone had been through so much, and we were all coping in so many different ways. I reached a hand toward her.

She dropped the backpack at my feet and took a step back.

"There's more in the back of my digger, and there's still more on the other floors of the core-scraper." She pointed at the backpack. "This is what I'm capable of. No more practices needed. We can fight and fight now. Finn, Mandeep, Jimmi, and you and me . . . We are ready."

"Let's stick to the raiding plan for now," I said.

"Yes, sir. If you say so, sir."

I pulled my hand back. "Thank you," I said finally. She turned and began to walk away when I added, "Thank you, Elena."

She stopped but didn't look at me.

"You're welcome, *Nichols*."

Then she turned her head slightly, and I saluted.

She smiled briefly, then turned back and walked away.

But she had smiled.

Maybe there was hope after all.

Chapter Sixteen
Reality

The next night, I was on watch, sitting a short way from the infirmary and reading my book. Oliver had just been shot during an attempted robbery. He was the robber, although he'd actually been forced into it by this jerk named Bill Sikes. Just as I got to the part where Sikes left Oliver for dead, I heard a loud rumbling echoing down from the direction of the elevator shafts.

I closed the book and stood up. The noise grew as I walked down the tunnel, listening intently. All of a sudden the rumble gave way to a tremendous thunderclap, and a cloud of dust flew at me, the force knocking me over.

Even as I flew backward, a thought hit me as hard as

the blast. The Landers had finished loading the ore and were detonating their bombs!

I scrambled to get up, and hurried in my digger back to camp. An avalanche of debris chased after me. Chunks of concrete and steel dinged off the rear of my digger. I turned on the radio and yelled, "Landers! Landers!" then ignited my disrupter and escaped into the rock.

We had an emergency plan already drawn up, which was basically to move camp as far away from the core-scraper as possible, then go back and see what had happened. I hoped I was wrong about the bombs because if that were the case, even moving camp wouldn't save us.

Everyone was awake and moving by the time I returned. Elena ordered them to grab their belongings and get into a digger. She'd already loaded Alek into her cockpit. He was sitting there, staring ahead.

Maria had gathered Darcy in her cockpit. I gave Darcy a thumbs-up. She smiled weakly but was trembling.

We turned on our diggers and sped farther through Tunnel 3 down into the mines.

My digger was in the lead, and I alternated two more series of left and right turns. Then my light illuminated an enormous excavator, sitting idle before a wall of solid rock. I slammed on my brakes. We'd reached the end of the tunnel. I realized with a pang of sadness that this was where the miners had stopped digging the night before the blackout party.

There weren't even any lights, emergency or otherwise, this far down.

I flicked on my microphone. "Okay, we'll set up the sleeping quarters near the excavator, where it's dark. Mandeep and Finn will help set up camp. Elena and Jimmi, once you've dropped off your supplies, we should head back to the core-scraper."

"Roger," Elena said.

"Okay," Jimmi said, but I could hear his quick breathing through the speaker.

Half an hour later we returned to the main entrance to the tunnels. The hall was completely filled with a wall of concrete, steel, glass, and garbage. It was like staring at a giant wall of junk. Small rivulets of dust and rubble trickled down the face. We could get to the other tunnels, but not back to the core-scraper.

"I don't think this was caused by a bomb," Elena said, pulling her digger close to the wall. "There's no smoke, no fire, no cinders."

I pulled up alongside. "So, a cave-in?"

She nodded. "A big one. Plus, there's still breathable air here in the tunnels, which means the terra-forming equipment is still working."

"We must have set off a chain reaction when we took out the twenty-eighth floor." My insides twisted. This was my fault.

"Maybe. But I doubt it. The core-scraper had been seriously compromised by the original attack. There had to be a lot of weight pushing down on that floor already."

"So it was just a matter of time before gravity finished the job."

She pointed at the wall. "This forces our hand, you know."

There was no way to go back inside the core-scraper or the hall. The cave-in had crushed the locker room, the infirmary, and the cafeteria, along with the refrigerated food inside.

"Why can't we just dig through the rubble and get the stuff?" Jimmi asked, his eyes darting around nervously from us to the wall.

"Doesn't work that way," I said. "When you dig in solid rock, the stuff above you isn't loose, so it doesn't fall down. Digging through a cave-in is like digging in sand. It will collapse."

Jimmi backed up a few feet. "It doesn't look very stable," he said, watching as small bits of debris came loose and fell to the floor, even sending pings of pebbles off the cockpit roof of my digger.

"Let's head back to camp and figure out a plan," Elena said. We backed up and turned around, heading down the tunnels in a line, Jimmi first, me in the rear.

I flicked off my radio and yelled, pounding my steering wheel. This was bad. In a flash, the only food we had left were the supplies we'd carried to the camp. We were going to need food and water, and we'd need them soon.

I'd been hoping to put off a real raid until it was absolutely necessary.

Now it was.

"It's okay. A cave-in, but not an attack," I said as I got out of my digger. Maria gave a huge sigh of relief. "But we've lost the infirmary and the cafeteria. I have a plan. Meeting in five minutes."

I walked over to Darcy. "Can you keep an eye on Alek while we have our meeting?"

She gave a serious nod. "He and I want to make toys out of the used food cans."

That was a bit of a surprise, a happy one. "Cool! Be careful you don't cut yourself."

She nodded again and toddled off to the beds.

Mandeep gave me a quick smile. "Alek still isn't saying much, but he does seem to come alive a bit with Darcy and Finn."

"That's good."

"And a little more good news. While you were gone, we took a look around. There's actually a break room just up where the lights still work. No food, but they did hook up some water. And they predug holes for toilets."

"Great. Thanks. Tell everyone we'll use the break room for the meeting." I walked off to see how well the predug toilets worked.

A few minutes later everyone had crowded into the room.

"Okay. The situation is this . . . ," I began. "We just lost our main supply of supplies."

There was a collective groan.

"There's good news. There is a place filled with supplies from Earth and food from the farming zones here on Perses. The main storage depot."

"Isn't that where the Landers are?" Maria asked.

I nodded.

"A full-out attack could get us enough food for the rest of the Blackout," Elena said.

"But if we attack, won't they come after us?" Maria shuddered as she said this.

"We don't even have any weapons," Jimmi said, his voice rising.

"I know, I know. But when we say attack, we don't mean an actual *attack*." I stared at Elena, hoping my use of *we* would make her understand the others still weren't ready to think about a fight, let alone have one. "What we're talking about here is more of a raid. We think there's a way to get in and out without them knowing we were ever there."

"How?"

Elena took a bit of concrete and began to draw a circle surrounded by small dots on the rock wall. "This is the layout of the main depot. The circle is the landing pad and the administrative buildings, the hospital, that sort of thing. These dots are storage silos. Like the core-scrapers, the silos are built down into the ground." She drew a large X about a foot away. "And this is our location."

I drew a line from the X to the circles.

"We can stay underground, undetected. We drive the diggers right underneath the storage silos, make a hole, climb up, grab some food, and head back out."

"What if there are Landers inside the silo?"

I jumped in before Elena could say how much she looked forward to that. "There won't be. I don't think they know there are survivors, or they don't care about us enough to come after us. So they won't be guarding the food."

"Which one is the food silo?"

Elena drew a large circle around the whole image. "I've gone with my dad on trips to the depots. The ones near the landing pad hold all the ore. The food storage is kept away from those to prevent contamination. But I've never actually been to the actual food silo."

Pavel snorted. "Let me get this straight. We don't even know where to look?"

"Not true," I said, sensing a brewing argument. "The Landers have to eat. They have a large crew. We all saw that. So they have to feed them, and there is no way their ship is giving up storage space for food they can steal here."

Elena nodded. "So, we monitor their movements around mealtimes, and see where they go on a regular basis."

"How the heck do we do that?" Jimmi asked.

All eyes turned to me.

Elena and I sat in our diggers. We were the guinea pigs, in a way. If this raid worked, it would be the template for all future raids.

It was a risky plan. I couldn't see Elena through the rock, but I knew she sat exactly five feet to my left. Our radio receivers were on, but our microphones were off. The Landers were only a few feet away, traversing the ground right above us. The sensors in our diggers could pick up the vibrations from their vehicles. We'd slowly snuck underneath one of the roads that led to the main loading dock, where we assumed the Landers' ship was sitting.

And we were waiting.

There were numerous roads that radiated out from the central landing pad. There would be lots of heavy traffic above us all day long, the transport vehicles moving ore from storage silos, and the processing machines, to the ship.

We were ignoring that noise, looking for something smaller. We'd been here for most of the day, and a pattern was emerging. An hour or two before each meal, a small vehicle, judging by the smaller vibrations, would set out and return on the road directly above us. It was a couple of hours before dinner, and if the sensors picked up the same vehicle, we were going to follow it.

The sensor on my dashboard began flashing. The smaller vehicle was making another trip. "Bingo," I said.

I turned on my radio and tapped three times on the microphone.

Elena tapped two times back and restarted her disrupter. She drove straight ahead, staying right underneath the vehicle. It began to slow, and so did we.

I watched the screen. The vehicle continued for another thirty feet or so and then stopped. A few minutes later it started up again and headed back to the ship.

The cooks, if we were right, had just gotten their ingredients and were now heading back to prep dinner. I waited until the vibrations disappeared, then I tapped three more times on my microphone. Elena answered back.

I began to move forward and then dove down. After a drop of about thirty feet, I turned my nose up and approached the silo from the bottom. Elena was on standby in case something went wrong.

I didn't want to think about that, partly because there was no real plan B.

If I got in, and we were right about the silo, she'd also break in but from the side.

My digger crept closer and closer, until the nose cut through the concrete floor of a dark room. The sensor on the nose cone kicked in and stopped the disrupter. I continued to drill ahead slowly, as quietly as I could, and emerged in the silo. As soon as my cockpit was above the level of the floor, I turned off the engine. I opened the latch a crack, not enough to turn on the light, and listened. There was no sound. The room was completely dark and very cold. There was the faint aroma of cooked food.

I smiled.

I crawled out of my cockpit and turned on my head-lamp. A package of hams had caught on the disrupter. It was steaming and smelled delicious. I could hear the sizzle of the roasting ham but nothing else.

My stomach growled. But I wasn't here to eat. I was here to be the Artful Dodger.

I reached back in my cockpit and turned my radio back on, tapped the mic three times, and then turned it off.

A few moments later the nose of Elena's digger cut through the wall to my right. Then she spun around and backed in, opening the storage area at the back of her digger.

I quickly grabbed as much food and water as I could. I also grabbed the hams, stealing a small deliciously crispy bit of gristle before I placed them in Elena's trunk.

Elena gave me a wave and then drove away slowly.

My nerves were on edge, half expecting the sound of the door opening, or somebody coming back because the cooks needed an extra onion. But I pushed all the fears out of my head and concentrated on covering our tracks. Luckily, the diggers didn't leave much rubble in front of them, so I just needed to disguise the holes.

I slid a stack of boxes in front of the hole Elena's

digger had made. Then I put a large crate next to my hole. I got in my digger, reversed down about ten feet, and then dug back up on an angle. Once my cockpit was even with the hole, I stopped and then flipped it open. Standing on the fuselage of the digger, I reached back into the room and grabbed the crate. I slid it, as best I could, over the hole my digger had cut in the floor.

I knew the holes would be found eventually, but I hoped we'd be able to stage a few more raids before that happened.

I turned my radio back on and tapped it three times. Elena tapped twice, and I heard her give a huge sigh of relief. I turned my mic off, and we headed away.

About five minutes into the return journey, I noticed a red blip on my screen, a warning signal.

It hadn't been there thirty minutes before, and I was now following almost the exact same path back from the food depot.

As I watched, the red blip became more constant and brighter. My screen was now showing at least thirty red blips, all from the same place.

Had I stumbled on my dad's warning beacon? This was too good to be true. I quickly noted the coordinates. Then the red lights shut off.

I shook my head, just in case I had hallucinated. How could they just disappear like that?

I turned on my radio. I hoped we were far enough away from the Landers that there was no way they'd hear us, even if they were listening for radio transmissions, which I doubted. Still, I kept it short.

"Miner Three to Miner Two. Detour. See you at home."

"Roger, Miner Three. Miner Two out." There was a pause, and then I was sure she added. "Be careful." But it was barely a whisper.

I turned off my radio and headed for the location of the blips.

That many signals together could signify a tunnel that wasn't on our maps, or a huge seam of volcanic rock, one it could take me an hour to drill out of without my disrupter.

On the flip side, if it was my father's beacon, why did it turn on and then turn off so suddenly? I didn't want to risk plowing into it by accident before I could find out. Either way, I needed to be careful. I slowed to a crawl.

The red blips started again a minute later, closer but all together. Then they stopped again. I sped up a little and broke through the rock into an open space. The disrupter shut off, and I eased onto the carved rock floor.

The main lights were on. I stopped the digger and

hopped out. I was standing in a tunnel—a really big tunnel. It curved away from me about a hundred yards on either side. The ceiling was a good forty feet up. It was more like a big room, a grand hall, about twice the size of the locker room in the basement under our building.

Was this supposed to be the foundation of another core-scraper? A storage locker for more ore?

A regular clicking sound started echoing from somewhere up ahead, around the turn. The signals were firing again. I listened for a few seconds, walking slowly toward the sound.

I turned the corner and stopped.

At the end of the hall, about ten feet away from where I stood, was a huge steel cage. It was made from the same material as the caged storage locker in my basement, but this went from the floor to the ceiling.

The closest wall was lined with bunk beds, and on each bed was a kid.

I counted four as I crept up slowly.

The children's eyes were closed. They were dirty. They looked sick. More than a few looked like they might be on the verge of starvation or dehydration. One boy's chest was barely rising and falling. His arms draped over the side of the bed, dangling and motionless.

I reached the cage and saw one of the beds was empty. The clicking noise resumed, and it was coming from near my feet.

I looked down. A girl about my age was lying on the floor, leaning against the locked gate of the cage. Her eyes were barely open, and her lips looked so parched, I thought they might crack. She was holding on to a long rope. It was made of slits of fabric that had been ripped from sheets and then tied together. A hook at the end, made from a pair of glasses, was caught on a box.

She'd caught the box and then dragged it toward her.

I got on my knees and examined the contents. It was filled with small red discs. They were blinking, clicking, and then they shut off.

I touched the girl's hand. It was freezing cold. "My name is Christopher Nichols," I said. "I'm a miner."

Her eyes focused on me, and in a hoarse croak she said, "Hello, Christopher Nichols. My name is Fatima Carvalho. I'm a grinder."

Chapter Seventeen

Ground

Fatima's head rested on my shoulder as we flew back to the camp. She had used up all her energy grabbing the warning signals, and she needed medical help, and fast. I left food and water from the raid with the other grinders.

Grinders.

The word shot through my brain like an electric shock. A *grinder* was a person. No, not a person, a child. I thought—I'd always been led to believe—that a grinder was just another piece of mining equipment. A machine. But a grinder *wasn't* a machine.

A grinder was a kid.

I shook my head. I needed to focus on getting Fatima to Mandeep. I flicked on my radio, hoping I was right that the Landers weren't listening.

"Miner Three calling."

Elena answered. "Miner Two here, go ahead."

"Elena. I need Mandeep to get ready. I've got an emergency."

"Christopher, are you okay?" Her voice cracked.

"I'm fine. But I've got a patient. A grinder."

"A grinder? Isn't that a machine? How did you fit one in the digger?"

Elena didn't know. I felt a tinge of relief.

"A grinder isn't a machine. It's a sick girl, and she's in my digger right now."

Elena didn't say anything. I could hear her stumbling for words.

"I can explain later. Just tell Mandeep to get ready. Food, water."

"Um, okay. Roger."

Elena called out to Mandeep before turning back to the microphone.

"Doctor says to make sure she doesn't fall asleep. Keep her talking, active."

"Got it."

"Roger, and out," she said.

Fatima lifted her head and opened her eyes. Good. I had lots of questions.

"I thought a grinder was a machine."

Fatima gave a small laugh. "That's what they want you to believe."

"But why use kids?"

"Machines are expensive. Expensive to build and expensive to ship into space. Children had been used in mines for centuries, so they went back to what worked." She coughed and then put her head back on my shoulder.

"What does a grinder do?"

She lifted her head again. "The jobs that are too risky for an expensive machine or a fully paid miner."

"Like what?"

"We can crawl into small crevices and holes encrusted with delicate gems, gold, platinum. Dig, dig, dig. And pray there is no cave-in." Her head lolled again and fell back onto my shoulder.

I felt horrible making her concentrate, but we still had ten minutes to go, even at top speed.

"Are all the grinders children?" I asked, dreading the answer.

Fatima nodded. "Small hands and small bodies. Also small price tags. My parents barely got a month's rent when they sold me to Melming."

I gripped the steering wheel so hard, my knuckles hurt. "That's horrible."

"Yes. But in some ways it is better than growing up with a family like mine. I escaped them. You can't even imagine, can you?"

"My father was a miner," I said, bristling.

"Look at your smooth hands, your clear skin. You've never done a hard day's work in your life, rich kid. That's why your shoulders are so soft, like a pillow. I need to sleep."

"I'm sorry. I didn't know."

"And if I survive a few years, then I get my freedom and even a little money. Do you have any water?"

I reached under my seat and pulled out a bottle, handing it to her. She took just a little sip, then three more small ones. "It's not a good idea to drink too much when you are dehydrated. I've seen the pain and cramps that can cause."

"How long had you been down here?"

"Two years. But there were other grinders before us. Once they grow too big, they are sent back to Earth, and then more children are brought here. There are always children."

I closed my eyes and shook my head. I'd seen transport ships arriving, but my parents had always said they were bringing new supplies. Was that what Fatima was to Melming, to my parents—a supply?

"How long had you been locked in that cage?"

"Days. Days that seemed like an eternity. All your miners had gone to some party. They never came back."

They hadn't even invited the grinders to the party. They had just left them in a cage. I was having a hard time processing all this. I wasn't angry yet—just kind of in shock.

"We had some water and some food, but it ran out. So I made a hook to grab the beacons and hoped someone would track them to find us. You did." She took another sip from the bottle. "Why did they abandon us?"

I hesitated, unsure of the answer myself.

"I assume there was a terrible tragedy. Why else would a rich kid like you be driving a digger filled with food, with no adult supervision?"

"There was a raid. Pirates of some kind attacked us. We call them Landers. They killed all the adults. There are only nine of us left, all kids."

She nodded again and tried once more to rest her head on my shoulder. "I am so tired. Let me sleep."

I hated myself for asking the next question, but I needed to keep her alert . . . and I needed to know. "Did all the adults know about this? About you?"

She nodded, or possibly her head had just rolled to the side again. But then she whispered words that sent a chill through my body. "We worked alongside all the miners."

A lump rose in my throat. I couldn't ask another question; it was like my head was screaming, splitting apart from the inside. I was afraid to open my mouth.

As I drove on, the depths of this new horror began to sink in.

My father knew about this.

My mother knew about this.

Hans Melming knew about this.

This was our Great Mission?

The other kids had called my dad and mom heroes. They had saved so many children. But had they, really? Or had they only helped their own? Had they let some children suffer, even die, working in mines? I felt sick.

We were almost at the camp. Fatima had fallen asleep on my arm after all. Answering the questions had spent the rest of her energy.

Mandeep was ready when we arrived. I gently lifted Fatima from the cockpit and laid her on the makeshift bed of blankets. Mandeep had an IV ready with fluids. I held Fatima's hand as Mandeep put the needle in, and while she woke up, she barely reacted to the jab. But her breathing was close to normal, and Mandeep told me that was a good sign.

I touched Fatima's forehead. She was cold. I couldn't imagine the pain she'd been through in the past few days, in her life. I leaned over and kissed her forehead. I wasn't even sure why. It just seemed like the thing to do.

She gave a weak smile and then fell back asleep.

I stood up and spied Elena a few feet away. She was watching, her arms crossed, her brow furrowed.

I turned to talk to her, but she spun on her heels and marched away.

I wondered if she recognized Fatima. How much did she know about the horrible underbelly of the Great Mission?

The question could wait. The other grinders couldn't.

I called an emergency meeting. Elena didn't show up, but time was very tight so I started without her. I asked everyone to sit down while I explained what I'd found and the urgency of getting back. Then I stood up.

"Okay, everyone, let's get the rest of the grinders!"

I expected the others to rush to their diggers, but they sat there on the floor staring at me. Finally Pavel raised his hand.

"Yes?" I asked, pointing at him. "You have a question?"

He nodded. "Why?"

"Why what?" I said, confused.

Pavel shrugged. "Why should we get them?"

My jaw dropped. "You think we should leave them to die?"

Pavel shrugged again. "Maybe, and maybe not. I'm just saying there are some questions we need to ask before we allow a bunch of strangers into our camp."

Jimmi and Maria nodded.

"Like what?" I said.

"Well, food, for one thing," Pavel said. "We've been rationing what we have, and adding more mouths isn't going to make that easier."

"But we just stole a bunch of food and water from the silo, and we'll go back and get more."

Jimmi frowned. "If we have to have even more raids, it just increases the chances of getting caught by the Landers."

"What are you saying?"

Jimmi stared at me. "I'm saying that Pavel makes a good point. Is helping them worth the risk?"

"We cannot let anyone else die who doesn't have to." I tried to sound as firm as possible, but I could hear the tremor in my voice. "We can't turn our backs on them."

Pavel shook his head. "But people do that all the time. I saw a movie once about a shipwreck. The lifeboat was full, but there were still people in the water who tried to climb in too. The people in the boat wouldn't let them. It sounds horrible, but if they had let them in, the boat would have capsized, and everyone would have drowned."

"This isn't a lifeboat. No one can sink in a mine!"

"It was an analogy," Jimmi said. "And I think Pavel makes a lot of sense."

"But these are kids just like us." I could feel my heart sinking deep into my chest. How could Pavel and Jimmi feel this way? How could they look at life so coldly?

Pavel leaned forward. "What do we even know about these grinders? Maybe they're nothing like us. You said they grew up in slums and stuff. Maybe Fatima is here to spy on us. Maybe they'll steal our food."

"They might kill us in our sleep and take all our stuff," Jimmi said.

"Yeah," Pavel said, nodding. "Maybe that's why they were in a cage. Maybe it was a jail cell."

"You already unlocked their cages?" Maria asked.

"Of course," I said.

"Then they're free. Let them save themselves. We did."

"But they're kids! When someone needs help, you help. Otherwise we're no different from the Landers."

They just stared at me, frowning.

"We can use them as cannon fodder." It was Elena.

She'd walked into the room without me noticing. I didn't like what she was saying now, but it got the others to turn away from me for a second.

"What do you mean?" Jimmi asked.

Elena stepped into the middle of the circle. "I'm saying they can be useful. They probably have a pretty good sense of the tunnels. We can use them as guides for now. And if it comes to a fight, we can send them out in front. That's what armies have done for centuries. Use the least valuable people up front."

I tried to catch Elena's attention to see if she could really be suggesting something so brutal, but she refused to meet my eyes.

I watched as Jimmi nodded. Maria and Pavel did too. Elena continued, "Bottom line is that we can't just leave them to die. What if the Landers find them, or they find the Landers, and then they turn on us? They know we are here, and now they can go anywhere. Now that they are free, it's riskier to leave them."

Elena turned and looked right at me. Was she blaming me for helping them?

"I couldn't leave them caged up—" I said.

Elena waved her hand to cut me off. "The clear objective now is to minimize the damage and turn it to our advantage. Of course, that means we do have to go get them." She paused a moment. "If that's what our fearless leader thinks is best?"

I couldn't speak. I turned away.

"You do want us to go get them, right?" Elena said.

I nodded.

Elena clapped her hands. "Good. We're agreed. So let's get in the diggers, and go get them."

Jimmi and the others got up and walked out of the room, avoiding looking at me.

I stood there, my eyes closed, anger and confusion rising in my throat.

Elena looked at the floor. "You better suit up too, Nichols. The more diggers we have, the faster we can get them back here."

I looked up as Elena marched out of the room.

I slammed my hand hard against the wall, and followed her.

Chapter Eighteen
Illumination

One of the grinders didn't make it. The boy I'd seen looking so listless. I'd hoped the food and water I'd left behind would help him recover.

Mandeep had come with us and hurried to help him. She tried pounding his chest and giving him mouth-to-mouth, but it was too late. She looked at me, shook her head sadly, and covered him with a jumpsuit.

She examined the other grinders. There were now only four left alive. Fatima, another girl, and two boys. They were all too weak to even say their names.

Elena used her borer to drill a hole into the floor beside the cage. That left a pile of ground stone. She placed the body inside the hole and then used the rubble to fill the hole back up.

Elena took back the jumpsuit. She didn't say anything during the whole process, and silently handed Pavel the jumpsuit as she walked back toward her digger.

"We'll need it more than he does," Pavel said.

I wanted to punch him, punch him so hard his helmet would fly off. The fact that he was right didn't help me feel any better.

I walked over to the new grave.

I closed my eyes and said what I guess you could call a prayer. To whom and for what, I had no idea. It just felt like something should be said to recognize that this grinder had been a boy and had been alive. That counted for something. If it didn't, we might as well just surrender to the Landers right now.

Maria discovered a break room with some food and water a little farther down the tunnel. If the cage hadn't been locked, it would have been a five-minute walk for the grinders. We grabbed as much as we could. Then we fired up our diggers, shut off our microphones, and followed the coordinates back to the camp in silence.

Finn and Darcy had stayed behind with Alek to prep beds for the grinders, but Alek ran away as soon as he saw the injured grinders being lifted out of the cockpits.

I wanted to follow him, but Mandeep waved me over to help.

"Those kids smell," Darcy said as we laid the last of the kids on the cots. It was true. They had been trapped in cages with only a couple of buckets for a bathroom, and no running water. We'd at least been able to do some washing.

"I know. We'll help them clean up."

"Friendly thinks they're a little scary," she whispered.

"Well, they need our help. They are part of our family now." I said the last part louder, hoping everyone would hear.

I knew we needed to go over our plans, maybe even clear the air, but I just couldn't stomach talking to the others again. Elena's suggestion had gotten everyone to save the grinders, but had she been serious? I wasn't sure I wanted to find out.

I had an inkling that the ground rules had changed at that meeting, that Elena, if she wanted, could take over control of the group. Did she want to do that? I wasn't sure I wanted to find that out either.

I walked from the sleeping quarters, nodding to Finn and Maria who were on guard duty, back to the makeshift infirmary, which we set up a distance away down the tunnel.

Jimmi and Pavel had pulled out some cards and were playing a game, but they ignored me as I walked past. Fine. We'd deal with it tomorrow.

Mandeep was checking on the grinders, even chatting with the ones who were recovering faster. I caught the names—Julio, a quiet kid named Nazeem, and Therese—as Mandeep introduced herself and talked to them about treatment. Only Julio seemed well enough to answer. Nazeem occasionally nodded but said nothing. Therese was hooked up to an IV and didn't move.

Elena was nowhere to be seen. Maybe she'd gone to find Alek.

As I continued down the tunnel, I ran through the day again. Did Jimmi and Pavel and others have a point? Should we have left the grinders to fend for themselves? We were low on supplies. How would we survive with so many more people to feed?

I wondered what my parents would have done, but thinking of them made me angry. They had known about the grinders. They had known and done nothing. How could they have done nothing for kids?

Their copy of *Oliver Twist* was still in my backpack. The book had been helping me settle down each night. Now it seemed like a horrible relic of a happier but fake past, burning a hole in my back. I wouldn't read it again.

The irony of my parents giving the book as a gift for my birth, the birth of their only child . . . I could feel tears welling up in my eyes. I thought of my parents hugging me, teaching me, reading me books. My parents, telling me that we were on a Great Mission to save humanity while using kids as mining machines. Didn't they even read *Oliver Twist* before they gave it to me?

"You okay, rich boy?"

I jumped in surprise, then looked down.

Fatima was lying on her bed, propped up on a pile of uniforms, her eyes open.

I'd been so lost in thought, I'd almost stepped on her.

"Sorry. Just a little exhausted."

"You look rattled."

"I'm that, too. You're bouncing back." She was. Her eyes were alert, her lips weren't cracked anymore, and there was even some color in her cheeks.

"You don't live in a mine your whole life without a strong constitution. Weakness is a death sentence."

"The young boy didn't make it," I said, lowering my head.

"Thomas. He was so small. He never adjusted to the

travel from Earth or to the life here. I think he was homesick."

"I'm so sorry for what my family did to you, to all of you. For using you all like that. It's not right."

Fatima just stared straight ahead. "So, now that you all know we're here, what are you going to do about us?"

"There's actually a bit of a debate about that right now."

She nodded. "It's always like that. There was even some debate in the cage about who should get what and when. Who should risk their lives trying to escape. People chose sides, or tried to until I came up with the plan to get the warning signals. It was not pretty."

"I told everyone that you are part of our family now."

She scoffed. "They didn't believe you, not all of them. I can see the looks in their eyes when they watch us. And who says we want to be part of your family?"

"Well, don't you think we can help you?"

Fatima looked at me with one eyebrow raised. She lifted her hands and held them out like the trays on a balance. "Let's see. Over here"—she wiggled her left hand—"there are four kids who know the mines like the back of their hands and have survived underground for years. And over here"—she wiggled her right hand—"a bunch of little spoiled brats running around, who've lucked out for a couple of weeks." She let her left hand drop to the sheets. "I'll go with this one: it's got more weight."

Fatima folded her arms on her chest and smirked. "Oh, I know you want me to be grateful that you saved us. It helps quiet your guilt."

I just stared at my feet.

She gave a small laugh. "I don't mean to be so mean. I am grateful. But I'm not going to bow down and serve you or anybody ever again."

"Don't you think we all have a better chance together?"

Fatima stared at me for a good minute, pursing her lips.

"Let's say we could work together, get along, share the food. That keeps us alive in the same way a rat in a sewer is alive. But you and I both know that we'll have to fight the Landers in the end. That bald kid who likes to pretend she's a soldier knows it too."

"Elena," I said quietly.

Fatima nodded. "And if it comes to a battle with the Landers, who gets the diggers and who has to fight bare-handed? Who gets used as cannon fodder?"

I looked at her, shocked.

She smiled and pointed to her ears. "You get used to listening for the smallest sounds down here. A trickle of water could mean a giant cave-in is coming. A distant echo off a tunnel wall could signal a digger coming straight for you."

"I don't think Elena meant it. I think she was trying to convince the others to move, to help."

"Maybe." Fatima nodded. "They did rescue us in the end. And that Mandeep seems very nice. Finn and Darcy, too. They gave me this." She held up a small cat, made from a tuna can. The edges had been filed smooth. "I like it. I've always wanted a cat. Once the others are healthy, we'll discuss whether we should save your butts, or not."

I nodded.

"Do you have any idea who the Landers are?" she asked.

"No. I know they are here for the ore. I know they are murderers."

Fatima stared at me. "You're quick to judge."

"How can I not? They killed everybody they saw. They'll kill us if they want to. Elena thinks we should kill them first. She might be right."

"Maybe they are desperate, and that's why they attacked."

"Isn't everybody desperate? That's why we're all up here, to save everyone back home."

"Maybe these Landers come from someplace poor.

Maybe they worry that Melming, and the rich nations of the world, despite their promises, won't be as willing to share? Have these Landers been corrupted by fear? Or greed? Or both?"

"You sound like my father," I said. "He was always suggesting something wasn't right with the setup of the mines, maybe with the world. He and my mom would get these looks sometimes. I thought he was just a worrier. Now, finding you, I know there was a lot more to it."

"Maybe he was uncomfortable with the arrangement. Not that he turned down the money," she added quietly.

That stung, because it was exactly what I'd been thinking. "Neither did my mom."

We sat in silence for a while.

"Do you hate me?" I asked.

"I don't hate. Hate does no good. I don't even hate Melming Mining."

"'We are what makes the Great Mission Great,'" I said bitterly.

Fatima took a deep breath. "Back in the digger I told you my parents sold me. They made a horrible choice. But they made that choice because they needed money, they needed to shed a hungry mouth from a large family. I don't forgive them, but I don't condemn them. If I hate anything, I hate a world that makes people make that choice." She yawned. "I need to sleep. Your shoulder is softer than these uniforms. Maybe I can rest my head on you again?"

I raised my eyebrows at her.

"I'm joking. But if you want to stay there for a bit, that's fine with me. Something about you does make me feel safe."

"Okay," I said. I wasn't sure what to do. Sit there, I guessed. I thought about the book in my backpack again. I thought about what Fatima had said about the world being gray. I'd started reading *Oliver Twist* to find out why it was so important to my parents. Maybe I needed to do that still.

I quietly slipped the backpack from my shoulder.

Fatima breathed softly beside me.

I pulled out the book. The flashlight fell out at the same time, and it dinged off the floor. Fatima stirred.

"Sorry," I whispered. "Stupid broken flashlight. I should have thrown it out."

Fatima looked at the flashlight and grabbed it suddenly.

"Where did you get this?" she asked, holding it up and flicking it on and off.

"My father. But it doesn't work."

She shook her head. "It works perfectly."

"There's no light."

"It's a different kind of flashlight."

I must have looked confused.

"It's not for illumination, but for finding hidden trails inside the crevices."

"Oh," I said, not entirely sure what she meant.

"We don't have lights in those holes, like the miners do in the main tunnels. So when we blaze trails in the seam, we make dots on the walls with a special paint. It can only be seen using this kind of light."

Fatima handed me the flashlight. "This is very old. The ones we use today are much smaller." She pulled one out of her pocket and showed me. It was barely the size of a pinky finger. "Why did your father give this to you?"

I didn't answer. My mind raced. Maybe there had been no physical map to lose after all?

Had my father left a trail of dots on the tunnel walls? Was I supposed to use the flashlight to find them and follow them? That could take forever.

No. My father had said there was a map in the backpack. He said I'd need the flashlight, but I'd assumed that meant I'd need a light to read in the tunnels.

I flipped the book open to the front cover and shone

the light on the page. There was nothing. I tried flipping through the book, from front to back, but still saw nothing.

"What should it look like?" I said, panicking.

"Purple. But it's too bright in here. You need to be in the dark to see the markings." She offered me one of her blankets.

I threw it over my head and hunched over the book to block even more of the light. I smiled. This was how I read most nights in my room. I could almost hear my mom telling me to go to sleep.

Nothing appeared on the first few pages. I kept turning. Then I saw it. A purple circle in the upper right corner of page four. The circle was around the page number. I scanned the rest of the page, but that was it. I turned page after page and found more markings, always around the page numbers.

Some pages had one circle around the page number, some two. Some had a box, and then some had an X through the page number.

In the end I had discovered a series of numbers. That was it. Nothing to tell me what they meant, or what sequence they represented, or didn't. I grabbed my pen and scribbled down the numbers on the back cover.

Circled

4

15

38

56

Two Circles

5

7

9

12

Xed

6

8

37

55

And surrounded by boxes—47, 283, and 371.

Obviously it was a code, but what kind of code?

I flipped through the book again. There was nothing else.

The first few page numbers weren't even from the story itself but the introduction. Some pages mentioned parts of London; some didn't mention anything at all.

There was no pattern. My dad believed I'd find the numbers eventually, so there had to be a way to decode them on my own. My dad liked to call me a genius, but I knew I wasn't, not really.

I took off the blanket. Fatima was fast asleep. I lay on the cold floor and put the blanket over both of us. Then I shifted my helmet over my eyes to block out the light.

The numbers swam in my head, moving around in different orders and sequences. I watched them, seeing if they would combine to form coordinates, or possibly a series of numbered tunnels, like I'd used with Alek. Why had my parents made the code so obtuse?

Tomorrow, I thought, *I'll ask the others if they have any ideas.*

Before long, I was fast asleep as well.

Chapter Nineteen
Mapped

"Reveille! Rise and shine, lover boy."

I slid off my helmet and peered, the light making me blink. I wiped the dried spit from my cheek and waited for my eyes to adjust.

Elena was standing over me, tapping my ribs with the toe of her boot. "Get up. Time to give some marching orders, Fearless Leader."

I looked over to my left. Fatima was still sleeping. I'd only meant to take a short nap, but I must have slept for hours. Of course, it was hard to tell down here.

"Is it my turn on watch?" I asked.

Elena snorted. "Maybe three hours ago. No, you missed your shift. I took a double. You owe me."

I took a closer look at Elena's face. She was trying to sound light, jokey, but she looked tired, drained. Her eyes were red.

"You don't look like you slept much," I said.

"Christopher Nichols, you sweet talker. Did you try that line on her?" She jerked her head toward Fatima.

"What does that mean?" I said.

But Elena walked away, waving her hands to dismiss my question.

"I called a breakfast meeting, sir. We all need to talk."

I got up as quietly as I could. My head was swimming and groggy as I made my way to the storage room. Pavel, Jimmi, Maria, and Mandeep were already there. I could feel the hostility radiating from the group as I walked in. The fact that everyone was eating cold beans and canned corn didn't help their moods.

I wished Finn were there; I needed a cheering section. But he was probably keeping an eye on the grinders or Darcy or Alek.

I sat down, and Elena passed me a can of tuna and a fork.

"Hey, everyone. I am sorry I was so abrupt yesterday. I need all of you to feel you can voice your opinions openly. I was too dismissive."

Jimmi and Pavel glared. Maria let out a long sigh.

"But I do still say the grinders need our help. They can help us as well."

Silence, except for the sound of chewing.

Elena looked around the room and stood up. "The grinders are with us now. We can use them. What we need to do is to go on one more raid, but a big one with more diggers. Then we can assess what we can or cannot do as a group. And we'll get enough food to feed all of us."

Elena went on. "Nichols is right. The grinders can be useful for navigating the tunnels. Who knows them better? Right, sir?"

I hadn't said that exactly, but I just nodded and then stood by quietly as Elena continued.

"So, once they are healthy, they will accompany us on our raids. One driver and one grinder per digger. The driver will approach the storage, and then the grinder will go in and grab the food. They can climb up the holes we've already dug and can do it quickly. If they get caught, *we* can escape."

Maria stared at her half-empty can of corn. "More of this? Just great." She let her fork drop to the floor.

Jimmi slammed down his fork. "This is stupid. If we take that much food, the Landers will discover it's missing right away. They'd have to. Then they'll come for us."

I glanced at Elena. This was her plan. Was she going to answer? No, apparently not. She just stood there, staring into space.

My mind raced. "That might be true. But . . . but . . . if we are able to seize enough food, then we can store some, and then change our strategy for our next raids."

Maria raised her hand. "Meaning?"

Now Elena jumped in. "Meaning that we can then turn our attention to actual attacks. We can't avoid it any longer. This is a war."

I stared at her, incredulous. She'd manipulated the meeting to support her original plan to attack the Landers directly.

I tried to steer things back my way. "And by attack, we mean slow them down."

Elena nodded. "Tactical incursions against their primary operational capabilities." Everyone blinked.

I wasn't 100 percent sure what she meant either, but I added, "We can't let them leave before the Blackout ends. If we do"—I paused for effect—"then they'll blow everything up and leave us to die."

That sent a current throughout the room. It was the first time I'd said the possibility out loud.

Pavel practically jumped. "But what happens after the Blackout ends, if they're still here? They could still just kill us and make it look like an accident."

Elena shook her head. "They'd be risking getting caught by Earth's radar or satellites. Earth will be watching once the Blackout ends."

I nodded and took a deep breath. "And there's something else they don't know about."

Elena jerked her head toward me.

I pulled out the copy of *Oliver Twist*. "There's a beacon."

"Useless beacon, you mean," Elena whispered beside me.

"It was left here to signal Earth if there was trouble on Perses. My father told me about it before he died. He gave me a map, but I thought I'd lost it. I hadn't. I would never have discovered the truth if it hadn't been for Fatima."

I held up the book. "This is the map."

Elena still whispered, but with more of an angry edge than before. "Why didn't you tell me you found it?"

"Later," I whispered back.

"So, what are we supposed to do with this beacon, exactly?" Maria asked.

"We need to wait until the Blackout is over. Then we signal Earth that we need help."

"Why wait?" Pavel asked. "If those grinders can help us find it, then let's fire it now."

I shook my head. "We don't know what kind of signal the beacon sends. It might only send one burst, which will be totally wasted if we fire it now. It might be a coded secret channel, but it might not. So the other concern is that if we set it off now, the Landers will hear it. If they find it, I'm sure they'll destroy it."

"Aren't there other ways to signal Earth?" Jimmi asked.

"The Landers control all the communications up above. They'll blow that up, if they haven't already. Then we'll have no way to tell Earth we need help."

"What kind of help can Earth send us?" Maria asked.

"Better food, I hope," Pavel joked.

"Best-case scenario, we've delayed the Landers so long that they stay past the Blackout. Earth comes and attacks them. We get saved. Worst case, the Landers blow up everything, and Earth at least knows about it and they get caught."

"But we'll be dead, right?" Maria looked panicked.

I let out a long slow breath. A thought had occurred to me as we'd talked, a good thought. "Not necessarily." I started running some numbers in my head as I went on. "Actually, if we can slow them down, even if they do leave and blow everything up, we can survive without water and the other terra-forming equipment for a few days, possibly weeks. Probably weeks."

I was no dummy. I knew this wasn't exactly going to go over like announcing free birthday cake, but I'd hoped it would cheer everyone up a bit.

Adding, "Then we can wait until a rescue party comes from Earth," didn't help much either.

Elena delivered the knockout blow to my enthusiasm. "That's only assuming the Landers don't know we're here, or that they let us stay alive after they leave."

"Yes. True," I admitted.

"So where is this beacon, exactly?" Maria asked.

I hesitated a second. "Well, I'm not sure."

"I though you said that was a map!"

"It is. But it's not like a normal map. It's more of a code. Of some kind."

I read out the list of numbers, and explained the bits about the circles, Xs, and squares.

"What the heck does that even mean?" Pavel said, throwing up his hands in frustration.

"I . . . I don't know."

"Useless, like I told you," Elena said quietly. "It's a map you can't read to a beacon we still can't set off for another month and a half." Then she added in a louder voice, to everyone else, "So, let's leave that aside for a bit, as exciting as it is, and get back to more urgent plans."

I waited for her to go on again, but she didn't. "Your turn, Fearless."

"Elena's idea to hold one giant food raid seems like a very good one. We have enough to last about three weeks or so, but"—I paused and made a quick calculation in my head based on what I'd seen in the silo, and how much each digger could carry—"but another raid with more diggers will guarantee we won't need to risk more raids for at least three weeks after that."

"Which is when the Blackout ends," Maria said.

"Yes. But Elena is right. This is just a raid. The next operation will have to be some kind of attack on the Landers themselves. So, we need to be careful. We need to cover our tracks so we have some element of surprise for when we launch an attack on their—"

"Primary operational capabilities," Elena said. "So get your diggers ready. We need to set out soon."

"I'll go tell Finn," Maria said. "I think he'll want to come."

"Good idea," I said. "The more diggers, the more food we can grab. Thank you. I'll go ask the grinders to volunteer as well. Once they are healthy, we'll set out. Meeting adjourned."

As everyone walked into the tunnel to prep their diggers, Elena punched me in the arm.

"Ow! What was that for?"

"You said you needed my help. So the next time you have a map, or *had* a map, let me know."

"I'm sorry. I thought I'd lost the map, remember?"

"You still should have told me."

"I didn't want you to think I was an idiot."

"You failed."

"I said I was sorry!" I rubbed my arm. "By the way, thanks for backing me up about the grinders."

She looked surprised. "What else would I do? You're in charge. Now I need to go get my digger ready." She walked out of the room.

Elena said I was in charge, but she had gotten what she wanted. I wondered: Who was the real leader?

Chapter Twenty
Community

It took two days to get an answer from Fatima.

After the meeting, I'd laid out the whole plan to her, and explained the chance for grinders and minrs to work together on a raid.

Fatima had nodded and told me to go away.

Elena and Pavel then badgered me to force her to answer, or we'd go on the raid without them. I stalled, until, finally, Fatima summoned me to hear her decision.

Now I was standing in front of her, and she was clearly enjoying watching me squirm.

"I have met with my grinders and we have decided . . ." Fatima stood up, her legs wobbling. She rolled her shoulders, waved her arms, and shook her legs, wincing as each stiff muscle woke up.

I stood, staring at her, waiting for her to finish. She just kept stretching her muscles.

"You decided what?"

"Patience," she said.

She swung her left arm onto her right shoulder and began pulling it forward, grimacing.

"You explained we are equal partners in this raid, right?" I said.

"Patience." She grabbed her foot behind her back and pulled it up, sighing more than grimacing.

"Let me guess. You've decided to start a yoga group?"

She frowned at me, began shaking her arms and legs, then twisted her neck before giving out a long satisfied sigh.

Finally she put her arms on her hips and stared straight into my eyes. "We have decided that . . . we will go with you on this raid."

I smiled.

Fatima poked my chest with her finger. "But if even one miner leaves a grinder behind, no matter the reason, we will not just leave your camp, we will destroy it. Then we'll see who can survive the longest."

I opened my mouth to protest, but then shut it and held out my hand. "Deal."

"And I'm going in your digger," she said.

I nodded.

We didn't leave right away. Fatima said the grinders, especially Therese, needed a few more days to fully recover.

"Patience, rich boy," she kept repeating until we finally set out.

Elena ended up with Julio.

Mandeep offered to take Therese. Mandeep seemed skeptical that Therese was actually well enough to travel, and wanted to keep an eye on her.

The final grinder, Nazeem, went with Pavel. I shuddered a bit as I imagined how silent that ride was going to be.

Finn was going to stay back in the mines, alone in his digger, as a kind of backup in case anyone else's broke down or got caught in a cave-in. He seemed disappointed, but I promised him I'd find him more excitement later.

Maria said she still wasn't ready to fight, and offered to stay behind to watch Alek and Darcy.

"So, I'm out of this raid then?" Jimmi asked. He looked a little relieved.

Elena walked up and put a hand on his shoulder.

"I've got a better job for you. You can be our lookout."

"Lookout?" He gulped. "Is that dangerous?"

"Not unless you screw up," Pavel said.

Elena growled at him, then turned back to Jimmi. "It's easy. You need to dig just under the surface. Listen for any sign of a vehicle heading for the silo. We don't need to get caught red-handed in the middle of an operation. If it's all clear, tap three times. But if anyone starts heading toward the food, open your microphone and tap five times."

"Sounds good," Jimmi said, nodding and clearly relieved. He got in his digger and began cutting his way toward the surface.

It took us about twenty minutes to arrive. It had taken Elena and me more than thirty the last time, but Fatima had mapped out a more direct route that didn't involve turning off the disrupters for tunnels.

Jimmi tapped three times, and we approached the silo. Elena led Pavel and Mandeep toward the hole she'd made. Fatima and I approached from the bottom.

I was relieved to find that the crates Elena and I had moved were still blocking our holes.

We were able to move quickly.

The grinders expertly snuck through the holes and sent box after box of food and supplies down to the waiting drivers below. In only ten minutes we had filled all five diggers. Fatima and I slid the crates back over the holes, and we were off.

The raid was also successful as a team-building exercise, which was what I'd been hoping for.

Once we got back to camp, each cockpit opened, and a new conversation was added to the growing din.

Pavel and Nazeem were talking loudly about sports.

Finn was leading Mandeep and Therese in a stirring rendition of "Ninety-Nine Bottles of Pop on the Wall."

Elena and Julio were less animated, but were chatting about which can of food they were going to open first. Everyone began unloading and stacking the food in the storeroom, chatting, laughing, and enjoying their shared success. Maria and Darcy even came over to help out.

The only one who missed out on the camaraderie was Jimmi, who'd been all alone acting as lookout.

"Where is Jimmi?" I asked, looking around.

"Dunno," Pavel said. "He should have been back by now."

"Maybe he was waiting for some signal that it was time to head home?" Fatima asked.

"Argh!" I actually slapped my forehead with my palm. That was a detail I hadn't really worked out. Poor Jimmi was probably still up there, listening for Landers.

"I'll go get him," I said, walking back to my digger.

"Wait, stop moving," Fatima said. She walked over to the wall of the tunnel and cocked an ear. "There's a digger coming. Slowly."

"I don't hear anything?" Maria said.

"No kidding," Fatima said. She put her ear right up against the rock. "He's not moving very fast."

"I'm hungry," Darcy said.

"Me too!" Finn said.

"Fine," I said. "Okay, everyone go get ready for a feast. And rationing is officially canceled for the evening. I'll wait here for Jimmi."

Nobody argued.

I sat on the floor and pulled out my book, but I was too pumped to concentrate, so I put it in my backpack and waited.

Jimmi's digger arrived a few minutes later, driving slowly down the tunnel floor. He pulled up outside the garage, and I ran over.

Jimmi's face stopped me cold. He looked bleary-eyed, like he'd just woken up from a deep sleep. He parked his digger and flipped open the cockpit.

"Hey," I said.

He didn't say anything, but he glared at me with a scowl.

I tried to sound cheerful. "The raid was a success. Everyone's having a big party down in the storeroom."

Jimmi took a look down the tunnel, but his expression didn't change.

"Yeah, whatever," Jimmi said. "You know what? I'm not feeling very well. I'm gonna sleep."

I put my hand on his shoulder. "Everyone is having a good—"

Jimmi slapped my hand away. "Just leave me alone!"

I took a step back. "Look, I'm sorry. I should have told you we were heading back. That's on me."

"Whatever." Jimmi walked past me without another word and trudged to the darkness of the sleeping quarters.

I felt like a total jerk.

I was still a little flustered as I made my way to the banquet, but the sounds of the party cheered me up. Everyone was sitting on the floor and on boxes, stuffing their faces with tuna fish, rolled grape leaves, and even sardines.

"And we've even got dessert!" Fatima yelled, holding up a crate filled with chips, chocolate bars, and pickles.

Darcy and Finn seemed to particularly like combining them together and then making faces at Alek, who almost smiled.

I took in the scene and gave a sigh of contentment.

Maria walked up to me. "Jimmi come back?"

"Yeah. But he's pissed at me big time."

"I'll go talk to him."

"No. I think he wants to get some sleep. You stay and have fun. I'll talk to him in the morning."

I saw Maria steal a look at Darcy, who was helping Finn make an ad hoc fondue using a flare and a can filled with chocolate bars.

Maria's lips trembled. "Actually, I think I'm going to call it a night too." She walked out.

I sighed. Two steps forward, three steps back, as my mom used to say.

"Nice party," Fatima said, walking up and offering me some kind of canned hot dog in tomato sauce. I popped it into my mouth but had to choke it down. It was cold. "Next raid, we steal an oven," I said, gagging a bit.

She shrugged, tipped the tin, and poured the rest of the sausages into her mouth, chewing them as she smiled.

"So, maybe we aren't a family, but we're getting close," I said. "Sometimes you just have to dig a mile in another person's shoes and all that."

"When times are good, it is easy to stay close," she said.

I frowned.

She poked me in the arm. "But I do think this raid has made some progress. Good work."

I poked her back. "You too."

I looked up. Elena was staring at us from across the room. She wasn't laughing. She turned and said something to Therese and then left the room.

I was going to follow her when Darcy came up to me and tapped my leg. "Christopher. Do you like seafood?"

"Um. Yes. Why?'

She stuck out her tongue, which was covered with bits of half-chewed pickle and chocolate. "See. Food," she said, giggling.

Fatima laughed so hard, a bit of hot dog flew out of her mouth and skidded across the floor. Finn and Nazeem erupted with laughter. I looked over at them. Finn was doubled over and pointing at Alek.

Alek tried to appear innocent, but the more they laughed, the more his face broke out in a mischievous grin.

But Darcy wasn't done yet.

"Fatima is very nice," she said.

"Thank you," Fatima said.

"Is she your girlfriend?"

Now it was my turn to almost choke.

"Um, Fatima is . . . ," I stumbled.

"Do you want her to be your girlfriend?"

"Um, well . . ."

"Don't you think she's pretty?"

"Yes, I mean, of course, but . . ."

Fatima just cocked her head and smiled. She seemed to be enjoying my puzzled stutter.

Our eyes locked for a second . . . for more than a second.

Her eyes were brown and deep.

I quickly looked away.

Elena walked back in the room, staring straight at me. I felt a pang of guilt but wasn't sure why.

"Look, Darcy. I'm friends with everyone here. Everyone except maybe *you* right now, that is."

She looked hurt.

"Humph," she said, turning and walking back to Finn.

"Nice work, rich boy," Fatima said.

Chapter Twenty-One
Forked Roads

We took the next few days to clean up, take baths, and organize the food and water. Elena suggested we store food at different locations in all the tunnels. That way, if our home base was counterattacked and we had to leave our food behind, we wouldn't lose it all. She and Jimmi volunteered.

I tried to help Elena load up her digger, but she just shook her head. "Jimmi and I can handle it, sir," she said, reaching down to pick up a box of food. I reached out at the same time and grazed her hand by accident. She pulled hers away without looking at me and walked away with the box.

"You should probably be working on plans for an

attack," she called over her shoulder. "Time is running out, sir."

Jimmi walked up behind me, his hands filled with boxes. "What are we planning?" he said. "Sir," he added with a sly smile. At least he was now willing to talk to me.

"We need to slow the Landers down. We need to keep them here. And that means we need to attack their ability to move the ore from storage to the ship."

"Why not just attack *them*?"

"Good question," Elena said under her breath as she returned to the storeroom and grabbed another box.

I frowned. "Because we don't actually have any real weapons. Attacking a fully armed group of soldiers is a great way to get killed."

"So a surprise is best?" Mandeep asked, walking in and grabbing a box of medical supplies.

Finn was right behind her. "Surprises? I love surprises! Is it somebody's birthday? Is there cake?"

Darcy appeared out of nowhere and began chanting, "Cake, cake!" Then she stopped in front of me and stared expectantly, a huge grin spreading from ear to ear.

The mere mention of cake seemed to draw everyone else like a magnet, and within seconds I was surrounded.

"You know something," Julio said. "I've never had cake."

"Me neither," said Nazeem. "I can't wait!"

"Yes!" said Therese.

I stared at their rough hands and thin bodies, and I believed them.

I rubbed my temples. "I hate to say this, but there *is* no cake."

Darcy frowned, stamped her foot, and marched back to wherever she'd come from.

Julio and Nazeem looked at each other and then at me. They looked deeply disappointed.

I had an idea. "There's no cake, but there are some pies left over from the first raid."

Darcy reappeared out of nowhere with the same big fake grin firmly pasted on her face again.

Julio, Therese, and Nazeem gave each other high fives and dramatically licked their lips.

A few minutes later we were all sitting against the tunnel walls, munching on pies.

I noticed with a bit of alarm that, without planning it, the grinders sat against one wall, and the minrs were up against the other.

I sat in the middle of the floor and tried to feel part of both.

I heard Darcy giggle and looked to see what was so funny.

Julio had stuffed a whole slice of pie into his mouth,

and seemed delighted despite the sticky bits of blueberry and apple that now dribbled down his chin.

Jimmi looked a little disgusted by this and made a show of using his fork to very carefully break apart his slice and lift the bites to his mouth.

Nazeem seemed to find this hilarious and began mocking him, sticking his nose in the air and lifting his pinkie as he picked a blueberry off Julio's shirt and plopped it into his mouth.

Maria gave an audible gag and put her pie down.

Therese and Fatima started laughing so hard, they had to grab their stomachs.

Pavel stood, looking like he was going to walk over and start a fight. I figured it was time to change the subject, fast.

"While we're all sitting here happily," I said, "let's go over some ideas for our next raid."

Maria groaned, but she stayed.

Pavel sat back down, and Fatima motioned for Julio and Nazeem to settle down. She actually cupped her hand over Therese's mouth to get her to stop giggling. Therese didn't stop, but at least Fatima kept it muffled.

I looked at Alek, who got the hint and led Darcy back down the tunnel. I waited until they were out of earshot.

"We've been lucky so far. The Landers haven't clued

in that there are survivors, or if they have, they don't care about us."

Elena jumped in before I could continue. "But we can't hide any longer. We need to move on to the next phase. It's a risk, but a strategically defensible risk."

"Agreed. Our best plan is to slow them down, make some small targeted strikes against their equipment."

"Make them suffer," Elena said. I watched Maria shudder, but Elena went on. "We target containers trucks, vehicles, any equipment they are using to take the ore from the storage silos and to the ship. We just need to locate them accurately."

"There is a labyrinth of tunnels that runs underneath the storage areas. There's actually a large hangar where the ore containers are stored," Fatima said.

"Can you guide us there?" I asked.

"Yes. I've been there. It's carved out of volcanic rock so that it's impossible for diggers to break through by accident."

Maria looked confused and a little scared. "Won't the ore be in containers up top, with them?"

Elena shook her head. "The ore gets dumped in the storage silos, loose. The containers don't get filled until a silo is full. They get filled down below, then the container and the truck get lifted to the surface."

"By an enormous elevator," Fatima said.

"Wouldn't it be easier to attack the elevator?" Finn asked.

Everyone looked at him. He slumped back against the wall. "I mean, trying to take out the containers individually seems like it will take a long time. The containers are stuck if we attack the elevator. Sorry, dumb idea."

I looked at him and smiled.

"It's a great idea. That's our target," I said. "By a show of hands, who agrees?"

It was unanimous. I breathed a sigh of relief. Finn sat back up, beaming.

Fatima and I sat in the cockpit of my digger, focused as we drove away from the camp. I had volunteered us to be the team to destroy the elevator, but I was nervous. We didn't say a word the whole time.

I used the disrupter to burn a straight line through the rock until we reached the large hall near the grinders' cage.

Maria broke through the wall behind us. She turned off her digger and opened the cockpit. Her job was to wait here in case we got into trouble. What she would do if that happened was a little unclear. Rescue? Fight? Run and warn the camp? It was hard to predict. I knew

Maria wouldn't want to go anywhere near the Landers, and I was just happy she'd agreed to come this far.

Jimmi was above us, looking out for Landers. To my surprise, he'd volunteered.

I promised I wouldn't forget to send him a "head home" message this time.

According to our schedule, he was just arriving at his post.

I waved at Maria and began driving away.

The tunnels were totally confusing to me, but Fatima had no trouble navigating us all the way to the storage area. We drove down a narrow one until a red sensor began blinking on my screen. It was coming from a few feet ahead, through what looked like a wall of rock.

"The elevator shaft," Fatima said, grinning. "It's picking up the movement."

I turned off the engine and waited for the movement to stop. A few minutes later the sensor went off, and I tapped my microphone two times, waiting for an all-clear signal from Jimmi.

"Fatima, what will you do when you get back to Earth?" I asked, trying to fill the time with something other than my racing heartbeat.

"I've always wanted to be a doctor, help people. Or

maybe a politician. I could start a grinders party, work for equal rights. As long as we're dreaming. You?"

"I wanted to be a scientist," I said. "Like Melming. Now, well, I don't know. What's taking Jimmi so long?"

As if on cue we heard three taps come through the speaker.

I took a deep breath and turned on the engine.

"Don't blow anything up," Fatima said, giving my hand a squeeze.

I eased the digger forward. We reached the concrete shell of the elevator shaft, and I fired up the disrupter. It was too noisy in the cockpit to talk, so we watched the rock ahead of us split apart.

Finally we broke through, just underneath the huge floor of the elevator compartment. The disrupter shut off. We turned and smiled at each other.

I drove forward and buried the nose of the digger into the elevator's giant hydraulic piston. Oil and metal flew all around, clanging off the walls and covering the cockpit window with thick black goo.

"We can't see!" Fatima yelled.

"No worries." I flicked a switch, and a tiny infrared camera in the hood turned on. "It sees through all that stuff using heat and radiation." A screen showed us what was happening outside as the digger continued to maul the mechanism that lifted the elevator.

It finally broke completely, and Fatima and I gave each other a high five.

I then angled the nose up slightly and began cutting into the elevator compartment. The borer was taking forever, so I tried firing up the disrupter. It burned against the metal for a short time before turning off. But it had left the beginnings of a hole.

I hoped the borer could finish the job quickly.

Sparks and smoke filled the screen, but the digger was barely moving forward.

"It's too thick!" I yelled. The digger was never going to cut through. And I was worried. The noise of the drill was amplified a hundred times as it rose up the elevator shaft. The Landers must have heard it. They couldn't call the elevator to come get them anymore, but I didn't want to stay in any one place too long to test that theory. I put the digger in reverse.

"Time to go!" I yelled over the noise.

Fatima nodded.

I reversed, and then we stopped. We didn't stop, the digger did. The lights all went out and the engine and drill went dead. I quickly felt for my helmet and flicked on the headlamp.

"What's the matter?" Fatima whispered. Her cold

hand grabbed my arm. I ran my fingers over the entire console. Nothing even flickered.

"We've run out of power. But that's impossible. The power cell was full when we left!" I had checked it, but somehow the long slow drilling with just the borer, and then the attempt to drill into the metal floor, had drained it. "The power got drained faster when we didn't use the disrupter to dig," I said.

It was a hard way to learn that lesson. We were stuck with no power, and no way to tell Jimmi or Maria to come save us.

"We've got to get out of here," I said. I pushed the button to release the cockpit, but it was dead as well.

"There has to be some way to open it manually," she said.

We searched for anything along the seam that might be a release latch or switch. Then I reached under the seat, and my fingers wrapped around a handle. I pulled it, and the roof opened.

Fatima and I crawled out. I heard noises from the shaft up above—muffled yells.

"I can get us out of here," Fatima said. "Follow me back down the hole."

I started to follow and then stopped. I turned and stared at the digger.

"We can't leave it behind. All the Landers would have to do was recharge the power cell, and then they'd have a working digger. They'd also have a map of everywhere we've been. They could come after us."

There was a loud bang as if someone in heavy boots had landed on the elevator floor.

"We need to go now," Fatima said.

"You go. I'll be there in a second."

"No," she said.

I didn't have time to argue. Something Fatima had said earlier clicked an idea in my brain.

The disrupter had its own power source. It wouldn't turn on in open air, but maybe I could trick it.

I grabbed the tool kit from the storage area and hurried to the front of the digger.

"What are you doing?" Fatima said.

"Blowing something up."

Fatima scurried down next to me. "What do you need me to do?"

"When I ask for a tool, get it to me quickly. Wrench."

She handed me one. I was able to open up the hood with a few strokes. I said a quick thank-you to the engineers who had made the digger engine both practical and easy to access.

"Screwdriver."

She dug around and then handed it to me. More boots landed on the elevator floor, and I could hear the loud hiss of something cutting through the metal.

I worked my way farther and farther into the engine block, taking out bits and pieces of the drive shaft and engine block that operated the borer. Finally I could see what I was looking for: a sleek box covered with yellow warning labels.

"The fusion core," I said in a whisper. This little box held the miracle that allowed the digger to work.

"The core," Fatima repeated. "That's what you're going to blow up?"

"Not exactly. Opening up the core won't do anything but poison you and me. It's not explosive, just radioactive."

A laser beam shot through the elevator floor, scorching the rock near my feet. I had to hurry.

I looked for the wires that ran from the sensor in the nose cone to the battery that triggered the reaction inside this box. I spotted it quickly, just as sparks began to cut a line through the metal above our heads.

"Wire cutter." Fatima handed it to me, and I snipped the wires.

I quickly jumped out from under the hood and reached into the cockpit. "Fatima, you get up into that hole now. I'm not sure how long we'll have once I flip this switch."

Fatima hurried away, and I got ready to run. I flicked the switch to ignite the disrupter. A high-pitched squeal filled my ears and the disrupter began to spin. A pale blue plasma enveloped the nose cone. It was beautiful, and deadly.

I bolted as fast as I could. Fatima held out her hand and pulled me into the hole. There was a loud clang behind us as the Landers cut through the floor, and a huge metal slab crashed into the back of the digger.

The squeal grew louder and louder, even as we crawled farther and farther away.

There was a deafening roar as the disrupter ignited the air, sending a huge fireball hurtling up the elevator shaft, but also toward us down the tunnel. The Landers had inadvertently given the reaction a whole new source of flammable oxygen when they'd cut the hole in the floor.

Fatima and I reached the main tunnel and sprinted. She led me into a side tunnel and then pulled me down on top of her. "Take a deep breath!" she yelled. I did. The fireball flew past the opening and licked the ceiling over our heads. I could smell the hair on the back of my head burning, and then the fireball spent itself.

We held our breath for a few seconds until we could feel cooler air come rushing back into the tunnel.

I rolled to the side and exhaled.

Fatima did the same. We actually laughed, from relief, but maybe with a slight tinge of the oddity of the situation.

Fatima reached out and stroked the back of my head. "No burns on the skin, luckily. But your beautiful hair, how sad."

My beautiful hair?

I got up and leaned into the main tunnel.

There was no sound of a pursuit from the elevator shaft—just the sound of flames, the dripping and sizzling of molten metal, and the crack of exploding rock.

The elevator was destroyed. There could be no question about that. The Landers who'd come to get us were dead. There was no question about that, either. My legs went limp, and I almost fell over as the shock hit me.

I'd killed someone. I'd done it to save my life and Fatima's and everyone's, but I'd still killed someone. I felt sick.

"Christopher, we have to go. We have to run."

I looked at her dumbly and nodded. Fatima grabbed my arm and pulled me along. I could feel the heat of the blasted tunnel floor seeping through my shoes, and the pain shook me back to life. I ran faster.

There was also no question the Landers up top would know we were here and that we were dangerous. They would come after us.

Chapter Twenty-Two
Burns

Fatima and I crammed together in the storage area of Maria's digger. We smelled too much like oil and burned hair to sit up front.

I kept going over the attack in my mind. It had worked, but we'd almost died. And people *had* died. "We did it," Fatima said to me, shaking my arm and smiling. "You did it, rich boy!"

We broke through the wall near the camp, and the others rushed to meet us. Jimmi had returned ahead of us. There were pats on the back and lots of questions. I said we'd have a full debriefing once we all got cleaned up, but no one wanted to wait for answers.

"Didn't you check the battery before you left?" Pavel asked.

"Lesson learned," I said. "Even a full battery will drain if you overuse the borer. And trying to cut through metal is not a good idea."

"You saw Landers?" Finn asked, more impressed than scared.

"Yes."

Fatima beamed. "And they saw us! We struck a pretty major blow to their operations, and they are going to be mad."

Nazeem seemed ready to run. "Shouldn't we move?"

"No, no," I said. "Finding us would be like finding a needle in a haystack."

Maria was holding her arms tightly around her. "But they can hurt us without attacking our camp, right?" Her voice was cracking.

"Possibly," I said.

"They could take out critical systems like water filtration," Fatima said.

"But they need those too, at least until they leave," I added quickly.

That sent a shiver through everyone.

"But the good news is that destroying the elevator keeps them here longer."

"Couldn't they just leave now?"

I shook my head. "This operation has cost them millions. There's no way they're leaving valuable cargo behind, unless they absolutely have to, and they aren't in that position yet. They've been here three weeks, and that's just not long enough to call it a success."

Pavel seemed unconvinced. "So, what do we do *if* they attack? Just sit here and die?"

"How do we get ready?" Mandeep asked. "Can we?"

Maria just rocked more quickly. "We can't fight them."

"We don't even have any weapons," Pavel added.

Everyone began talking all at once.

"We're sitting ducks."

"We have to attack."

"We can't attack."

"They're coming for us."

I held up my hands to quiet everyone down. "If we know they are coming, we can run. We have food hidden around the tunnels. We can survive."

"So how do we know when they are coming?" Pavel asked. "You a psychic?"

"We can have a permanent lookout. Instead of keeping watch in the tunnels, we'll send a digger up closer to the surface. If they pick up any movement, they can signal us and we can escape."

"So who gets that job?" Pavel asked, seeming to shrink back.

Jimmi raised his hand. "I'll do it," he said. "I've already done it twice, and it's kind of nice and quiet when you're alone up there."

"Good, thanks. Now, no more questions. I smell like garbage, and I need to wash up."

"That's no lie," Julio said. "And I work with Fatima so I know what a dump smells like!"

Fatima slugged him in the shoulder. "I can take a hint. I'll see everyone at dinner." I gave Fatima a hug, and she went to clean up.

Elena had been waiting the whole time against the back wall, watching, not saying anything. Everyone left, and she marched up to me with a scowl on her face. She didn't hug me, give me a high five, or even a pat on the back.

"You and Fatima make a good team?" she asked.

"She knows the tunnels better than anyone I've seen."

Elena flinched.

I tried to lighten the mood, so I turned around and pointed at the back of my head. "Look, I got the same haircut as you now!"

She didn't say anything.

"See? It was a close shave, get it?"

When I turned back around, Elena wasn't there.

My shoulders sagged, and I leaned against the wall, a wave of exhaustion and confusion and sadness hitting me at the same time.

Chapter Twenty-Three

Mixed Results

The Landers didn't attack that night or the next day or the next. That had me more worried than if they had attacked. It meant the Landers weren't worried about us. They were just going to speed up their work.

So we decided to lead another, bigger attack on their "primary operational capabilities." Fatima stayed behind this time, getting both grinders and miners prepped to leave at a moment's notice.

We approached in two groups of diggers. Elena was leading group one, with the goal of attacking the Landers' garage and taking out some of the big transport vehicles. The only problem was that we really had no idea where it was. She didn't seem worried. "Whatever we destroy will hurt."

Jimmi went with her in his digger.

I was trying something else.

None of us had spent much time in the docking area of the colony, but we'd seen it in bits and pieces. And we'd all arrived here through the landing pad. The main medical center, the processing plant, and the administrative buildings for the colony were there. We were all fairly certain we remembered one main ring road that connected all the silos to each other and then to the loading dock.

I was going to take it out, or at least a big section of it. Mandeep and Finn joined my group.

We couldn't break through the surface. That would leave us exposed. But we could weaken the ground under the road.

The risk this time was that we'd be doing our digging while the Landers were actually using the road. It was the safest way to mask any vibrations we'd be giving off. And we'd be giving off plenty.

We kept strict radio silence, but I had plotted a pattern into everyone's map.

We fired up our diggers and then began cutting, carefully keeping our directional arrows pointed straight ahead. We cut four parallel tunnels under a 200-yard stretch of the road. If my calculations were correct, there was barely a foot of rock left between the road and the holes we were leaving behind. I could even see cracks appear in the ceiling as I passed. Chunks of rock began to fall and ding off the hull of my digger. I nosed down just a touch. I didn't want the road to collapse while we were directly underneath.

My original plan was to come back and cut cross tunnels to further weaken the road, but now that wasn't necessary. I turned on my radio and tapped three times. The others tapped back, and we left. I kept my eye on the rear camera display and slowed. After a minute the huge track of a transport vehicle broke through the hole.

Mission accomplished.

We headed back to camp, washed up, and began prepping lunch.

I stared nervously at my watch. Elena was supposed to have gotten back almost at exactly the same time we had, but she hadn't.

Halfway through my lunch, Elena's digger finally shot through the tunnel, sliding and skidding. She threw open her cockpit and looked around the tunnel. She was hyperventilating.

"Is Jimmi here?" she asked. "Is he back?"

"No," I said.

She slammed her fist into the side of her digger.

"What happened?"

She leaned against her digger and rubbed her hand through her hair. "It started off well. We found a garage, collapsed a wall, and got out of there."

"You destroyed some transports?"

She nodded. "But then I had an idea." She stole a look at me and then lowered her eyes.

I winced. I had a bad feeling about where this was heading, but I let her go on.

"Jimmi was used to digging near the surface. So he agreed to try breaking through."

"What? Why?"

"It was just for a few seconds. We wanted to sneak a quick look at the setup to help us get some visuals of the ship, its location, the number of Landers . . ."

I began to pace back and forth in front of her.

"Go on."

Elena began to shake. "I don't know what happened. He was supposed to take some pictures and then join me back in the tunnel. I never got a distress call, so I assumed he was fine."

"We have to move camp. Fast," I said.

Elena didn't move. I didn't care. I turned back toward the storeroom.

Fatima was standing in the doorway. I wasn't sure how much she'd heard, but she was angry.

"Fatima, you and Mandeep prepped everyone?"

"Yes."

"Then let's move."

She nodded and hustled to camp.

I shook my head at Elena, who stayed glued to her digger, hugging her arms to her sides and staring at the ground.

There was a low rumbling from the wall. "Landers," I said, my eyes growing wide.

There was a blast of rock, and Jimmi's digger flew straight toward us, the borer spinning. I lunged and pushed Elena out of the way as the digger smashed sideways into her cockpit. The entwined machines careened across down the tunnel, sending out sparks before crumpling against the wall.

I ran over. The digger spit and smoked. There was a giant crack in the cockpit hatch, and Jimmi was trapped inside, packed in by dirt and rock. He was gripping his steering wheel, staring straight ahead, his face covered in grime.

"Jimmi, Jimmi!" He didn't answer.

I began clawing at the hatch. It gave, and I pulled the cockpit lid off. Then I began digging with my bare hands.

Jimmi kept holding on to the wheel, white as a ghost.

"Elena," I called. "I need help." I turned, but she was gone. Maria and Finn heard the commotion and rushed to help me, and together we were able to loosen the dirt enough to get Jimmi free. I had to pry his fingers from the wheel.

I laid him down on the ground. He was shaking.

Mandeep ran up and covered him with a coverall.

"Jimmi, it's Christopher. Are you okay? What happened?"

He didn't answer right away; he just closed his eyes. Mandeep took his hand and stroked it. He seemed to calm down, slowly.

"Good, good," she said.

"Jimmi, did you get any pictures?" I asked.

"N-n-n-n-n-n no," he sputtered. "I came up out of the ground and—and—and I was in the middle of a whole group of them. They had guns out and were running toward the garage."

"Why didn't you dive back down?" I said.

Jimmi closed his eyes again. "I panicked. I just sat there in the middle of them without moving, and then my disrupter turned off."

Jimmi trembled again.

"What happened next?"

"Once the disrupter turned off, I knew I had to run

for it. There was no way I could dig down fast enough."

Tears began to stream down his face.

"I knew the road had cracks in it from your raid, so I headed there. I just floored it and went right through them. I mean, really through them." He paused, sobbing.

"Jimmi, did they follow you?"

He took a few seconds to answer and then shook his head. "They just started shooting at me. They hit the digger again and again. I thought I was going to die."

"You're alive. You're safe now," Fatima said.

Jimmi shook his head. "I was able to reach the road, and then I dug into the rock. But they must have hit the cockpit because the rock just kept pouring in." He coughed, and his hand was covered in muddy mucus.

"That's enough," Mandeep said. "He needs some rest."

I got up and went to examine the digger. It was a total wreck. The camera and dashboard were completely shattered.

It could have been so much worse. The Landers hadn't hit the engine, or anything that would have stopped him and allowed them to capture a digger. And, of course, Jimmi was alive.

"Christopher," a voice next to me whispered.

It was Alek of all people. I hadn't heard him coming.

"Don't scare me like that!" I said, catching my breath.

"Sorry," he said. He was staring at the damaged digger. "Christopher, Jimmi looks sick."

"He was in a battle."

Alek nodded but was silent again.

"Alek, I know you've seen a lot. I know it hasn't been—"

"I'm okay now, Christopher," he said. "I'm better." As if to prove it, he pulled the tattered remains of the safety poster from his pocket and let it fall to the floor.

"They killed Brock, my parents, everyone I cared about. Right in front of me." He closed his eyes.

I put a hand on his shoulder.

Alek took a deep breath and continued to stare at the digger. Then he looked straight into my eyes. His were narrowed and sharp. "I want to help."

I probably should have said no, he wasn't ready, or wasn't prepared to deal with what our battles were going to be like now that the Landers were aware of us. But something in his eyes told me he wasn't asking.

Plus, with Jimmi dealing with his own trauma, we needed everyone to chip in, so I shook his hand and said, "Welcome back."

Chapter Twenty-Four
Leaks

I looked away from the diggers in front of me and stole a nervous glance at the small box on my seat. It was a power core for a disrupter. I'd salvaged it from Jimmi's digger and strapped a detonator cap to it with medical tape. It looked like a horribly wrapped birthday present.

I was going to use it to retaliate against the Landers. Not because we were angry, although we were, but because we needed to show them that we were willing to fight, even when we'd been fired at.

The detonator wasn't powerful enough to do much damage on its own, but if I could throw this little bomb into the food silo, it would spoil all the food the Landers had stored.

I reached over and touched the tape, being careful not to arm the cap. The box rocked a little, then settled onto the leather. I looked back up at the rear of Therese's digger. She had agreed to give digger driving a try after Jimmi's ordeal, and she was a natural.

Finn was driving just ahead of her. Pavel was heading to the surface near the camp to keep watch.

My radio crackled. "You're sure we'll have enough food if we do this?" Therese asked nervously.

I sighed. We'd been over this point.

"Yes. If we ration even a little, we can last the Blackout."

Finn came on the radio. "And I'll bet this is exactly the sort of the attack the Landers *don't* expect."

"Yes," I said, and silently hoped. "All right, we're approaching the junction with the grinder cage. What do you do next, Finn?"

"Therese and I split off and head in different directions."

"Good. Therese?"

"Then we make as much noise as we can. If the Landers are listening, we'll act as decoys. How about you, rich boy?" Apparently, Fatima had spread around the nickname.

"Then I sneak up the middle and deliver our little present."

"Good luck!" Finn said cheerily.

"Thanks. Now, radios off. We'll be there in five minutes."

There was a short buzz as the speakers turned off.

I ignored it. I shouldn't have.

The moment we hit the junction, there was a huge flash and a thunderous boom.

Therese keened to the right in front of me as debris shot back over us and down the tunnel.

Finn's voice came back at me, panicked. "I've been hit! There was a bomb!"

It was an ambush.

"Retreat!" I yelled, panicked.

Therese's digger stalled, and I turned sharply to avoid a crash. I ignited my disrupter and flew into the rock, turning again sharply to try to come out next to Finn.

My digger burst through the wall. Finn was just in front of me, sitting in the cockpit of his digger. It had been ripped to shreds. He was alive, but everything around him was on fire. He was strapped in and struggling to get the belt off his shoulder. He saw me and looked over, his eyes wide with panic.

"Christopher, help!" he said, desperately clutching at the belt as the flames grew closer to the cockpit.

Something moved in the tunnel ahead of him. Landers, dressed in black overalls, were approaching, guns raised.

"Finn! Hurry!"

They opened fire. Finn gave a cry and slumped forward in his seat, dead. More bullets flew, turning everything in front of me into a fireball.

I slammed my digger in reverse and flew backward, flames following me down the hole. My disrupter reset. I ignited it and disappeared sideways back into the rock, trying to get as far away as fast as I could.

Tears filled my eyes. Finn had been so happy to be on a raid. He'd been so excited to lead the charge.

If only I'd gone first, maybe I could have fought off the Landers, maybe I could have protected him. I punched my steering wheel again and again.

Finn had been the cannon fodder, and I'd been sitting behind, protected. I listened for Therese on the radio, but there was nothing. I hoped she'd escaped. If she'd gone into the wall to the right, she would be fine. If she'd stopped to help Finn, she was dead or captured.

I slammed on the brakes.

The bomb wobbled against my leg.

I stared at it, then gritted my teeth. The bomb. The bomb! I gunned the engine, spun the steering wheel, and turned back.

I broke through the wall, only about twenty feet from the site of the ambush. My digger landed on the floor with a crash and a thud. I spun and angled my nose back toward the wreckage. I pressed the detonator on the bomb.

Standing in a row, staring straight at me, was a row of Landers. Each was wearing a gas mask.

In a flash it hit me.

They knew.

They knew about the radioactive bomb.

They knew where we'd been heading.

They knew about our plan from start to finish.

And now they were going to kill me.

I was going to die.

The detonator began to blink red. I opened my cockpit and stood up. I threw the bomb just as the lead Lander raised his gun at me and prepared to fire.

It landed at his feet, but he stepped over it, advancing to get close enough for an accurate shot. I jumped back down, closed my hatch, and slammed the digger into drive. The digger hurtled toward the lead Lander, who hesitated a second and sent his shot into the tunnel wall.

Suddenly there was a blast to our left, and Therese burst through the wall. She slammed into the Landers, sending them flying like rag dolls. The detonator went off, filling the tunnel with fumes and smoke.

Therese didn't stop but drove right through the other wall, her disrupter slicing through at top speed.

"Follow me!" her voice crackled on the radio.

My disrupter was off, but I could follow. I quickly swerved to face the hole. I gunned the engine and darted inside.

Shots blasted the ceiling and the floor behind me, but they were firing blind, and I escaped undamaged.

As we flew deeper and deeper into the core, my mind was racing.

How could the Landers have known the plan?

They were clearly listening to our radios, and had tracked us in the tunnel. The buzz I'd heard had been a blip from their tracking device as they'd zeroed in on us. I flicked off my radio quickly.

But how did they know what frequency to listen to?

How did they know exactly which tunnel we'd be heading down? It wasn't just that the landmine had been in exactly the right place; it was also the fact that a group of armed Landers had been waiting there, prepped for both diggers and radioactive bombs.

That wasn't random chance, or an incredibly lucky guess.

And those weren't things we'd talked about on the radio, so how could they know?

There were only two possibilities.

One, they were able to listen in on our planning meetings and knew exactly what we were going to do.

Or . . .

Two: someone had tipped them off.

For a moment I suspected Therese. It had been her first mission. She'd known the plans. But I discounted this quickly. I'd seen the look on her face when her digger swerved. That was fear you couldn't fake. She could have left me for dead, too, but she'd risked her life to save me.

I flicked my radio back on.

"Therese, we need to stop."

"No. We need to get back to camp!"

"They might be following us. If they can track us back to camp, they'll kill everyone."

Therese didn't say anything, but I saw her digger begin to slow ahead of me.

"Let's find a tunnel, cut through, and then talk. Radios off."

We clicked our radios off.

A few minutes later Therese cut through the wall of a tunnel. It was unlit, which meant it was probably new and hadn't been attached to the power grid yet. I figured that was a good thing. We'd see the lights from anyone else coming a mile away.

We turned off our diggers and got out. I flicked on my headlamp. I felt sick to my stomach, but I needed to focus.

"We need to make sure we can't be tracked. Then we need to get back to camp."

She nodded. We searched our diggers for any trace of tracking devices. I wasn't even 100 percent sure what one would look like.

"It would have to be something small and that you could hide quickly. You'd need a lot of time and specialized tools to be able to put it inside the engine block or inside the hull."

We pulled out the seats and ran our hands along the inside of the trunk and hood, anywhere that you could gain easy access.

"Christopher, if we do find something, then that means someone had to put it there."

I nodded but just kept looking, convinced we'd find something, but we found nothing.

Therese gave a sigh of relief. I didn't.

"Just because nobody booby-trapped our diggers, it doesn't mean there isn't a traitor.

"It could mean the Landers found a way to listen to us back at camp," she said.

"But if that were the case, why not attack the camp? Or were they on their way and this attack was a distraction to keep *us* away?

"We've got to get back," she said suddenly, panicked.

"If the Landers know where the camp is, they'll be heading there now!"

Therese jumped back in her digger. I waved to her before she could close the lid.

"Let's keep radio silence until we get close. And don't mention anything about the attack. We need to keep everyone calm so we can move without panic."

"What do I say about . . . Finn?"

"We'll say he was brave. That he died in a cave-in as we were heading home. Until we know what's going on, we need to lie."

She gave me a nod, and we were off.

The quickest way for Landers to get to the camp was through the tunnels, starting from the storage depot. I assumed they'd have to attack on foot. The elevator had been the only way to get big machines belowground. They didn't, as far as I knew, have any diggers. So it would take them a while to find the camp in the underground maze. Even if they could pinpoint where the camp was, they would need to keep turning down different tunnels until they got there.

But if I was wrong, we'd be sitting ducks.

Pavel was listening for any sign of movement near the surface. He'd never even hear Landers marching underneath.

I had a sickening thought. Maybe we'd brought a homing device back with the food we'd taken from the Landers. Maybe they'd wanted us to steal the food?

We'd used our storeroom as the meeting room. If they'd been listening in, they'd have known everything we'd been planning, all the raids and all the places where we'd moved our supplies and spare diggers. All the ways we could possibly escape them if they did attack.

But that didn't make sense. We'd blown up a key elevator shaft after we'd stolen the food. Why would they let that happen?

I thought back to Coventry. Elena's lecture on how far a real leader was prepared to go to win.

Had the Landers allowed us to win one small victory in order to win the war against us?

Or had someone else?

But if there was a spy, who could it be?

Finn was dead. If he'd been the traitor, he'd been a bad one.

Alek was starting to come around but was still practically in a walking coma.

Jimmi had barely left his bed for two days.

Pavel? Mandeep?

The other grinders?

I ran through all the probabilities, and two names

kept rising to the top of the list, the two living people who probably meant the most to me in the world: Fatima and Elena.

Elena was always questioning my decisions. She'd manipulated the last few meetings to get her way and had devised much of the strategy. She knew every bit of our plans down to the minutest detail.

Elena had been up top for days after the attacks. What if the Landers hadn't overlooked her? What if they'd captured her and trained her, brainwashed her somehow?

What if she traded her life for the rest of our lives?

No. I wouldn't believe it. Elena would never do that.

Could Fatima?

If I were a grinder, I'd feel no love lost for a corporation that used me like that.

Fatima knew the tunnels like the back of her hand. She'd be able to give pinpoint directions to every stage of an attack. She'd been in the digger with me, and she knew what radio frequency we'd been using.

No. I shook my head. That was also impossible.

It had to be the Landers. They must have hidden a monitor or bug inside the food we'd stolen. They must have. I'd go back to camp and look. There would be some evidence. I'd find the bug.

I floored the digger and sped back to camp.

Chapter Twenty-Five
Nothing

The Landers were not waiting for me at the camp. I breathed a sigh of relief as I jumped out of my cockpit, trying to look as calm and collected as I could.

Therese had just pulled in before me and was still by her digger.

"We should get everyone ready to move," I said. "Go plug in your digger and make sure it's charged. Then go help Maria pack the sleeping stuff. Don't tell anyone anything yet. I'll get everyone ready."

Therese nodded. "I'm on it." She headed down the tunnel.

I did a quick walk around the camp.

Jimmi was in his bed in the infirmary, sleeping.

Alek was helping Mandeep organize the medical supplies for transport.

Fatima was sitting against the wall of the tunnel, reading. She stood up quickly and walked over to me. "You look wrecked. Did the raid go well?"

I shook my head. "Finn . . ." I choked up. "There was a cave-in. We got out, but he was crushed right in front of us."

"A cave-in? In the tunnel? Where?"

I tried not to look at her. If she'd set up the ambush, or if she hadn't, I was sure she'd know I was lying.

And if she was a traitor, I didn't want her to see any suspicion in my eyes.

I looked at the ground and waved my hand indiscriminately in the direction of the tunnel. "Later. I don't want to talk about it right now."

She took my hand and gave it a squeeze, but I just gave her a quick nod and walked away. "I need to go check on the supplies," I said.

I didn't look back. She didn't follow.

There was no sign of Elena or her digger.

She's just out for a walk, or she's doing some repairs on her machine, I told myself. *She's working out some new strategy for our next attack and wants to be alone.*

I walked into the supply room.

It was an odd feeling to hope to find evidence that your entire mission has been compromised, that you'd been sloppy when you'd brought something from an enemy camp straight into your own secret location. But that was what I was hoping for. I began combing through the crates and boxes we'd taken from the Landers.

I knew the bug would have to be something small and hidden but close enough to the surface of a container to pick up our voices. I tore open boxes, crates, cartons of dried goods.

Darcy walked in, clutching Friendly tightly. "What are you doing?"

"I'm just organizing the food into smaller bits. It makes it easier to move."

"We have to move again?" She looked a little scared. I walked over and gave her a hug.

"Where's Finn?" she said, looking around.

I suppressed an urge to cry. "I'm . . . I'm not sure." It was a horrible lie, but at that moment I didn't know what else to say.

"He's probably looking for Alek," she said, shrugging.

It took an incredible effort to keep myself together. I tussled her hair. She pointed a finger at me and said in a very serious voice, "Take the chocolate bars." Then she hugged Friendly and walked away.

I took a deep breath and got back to work, relent-lessly pulling apart the boxes. I didn't find a thing.

No bug.

That left only one explanation.

"Elena," I said. I put my head in my hands, drained.

What was I going to do now?

Mandeep poked her head into the room. "Christopher, we're ready."

I stood, but my legs wobbled and my head swam as I approached the waiting group. They were clutching their meager belongings.

"Before we all get in the diggers, I need everyone to come and grab as much food as you can carry. I've separated it all into cans and dry goods."

No one moved.

Jimmi asked the question on everyone's minds. "Why are we leaving?"

"We are in danger."

Now I hit them with more horrible news.

"Finn is dead."

Darcy was the first to cry. Then Alek began to sway. Mandeep reached over and grabbed him before he could fall.

"How?" Pavel yelled.

"Did you screw up the raid?" Jimmi said.

Julio and Nazeem looked at Therese who bowed her head and said nothing.

Darcy's howling grew louder. Maria, tears flowing, bent down and began to hug her, smoothing her hair.

"I'm so sorry," I said. "There was nothing we could do."

"Was it Landers?" Maria said, holding Darcy tightly.

I caught Fatima's eye. She was staring at me, still as stone.

"No," I said. "It was a cave-in. There are more cracks nearby. I don't think this location is safe anymore."

Fatima scanned the ceiling and walls, frowning. I looked away.

"Let's all calmly get the food stacked, and then we'll get the diggers and move camp."

"Where's Elena?" asked Pavel.

I'd hoped no one would notice that. "She's gone ahead. Scouting out the new area for us," I lied. "Look, I have to go prep the diggers. Stack the food here outside the storeroom. It'll be easier to pack the diggers here rather than carry everything back and forth."

"Yeah, now that you took it all out of the boxes," Pavel said with a huff.

I didn't have time for an argument. I needed to make a couple of preparations before everyone came to get in their diggers.

"We need to move. So let's hurry. I'll be back in a few minutes."

I made my way to the garage and leaned into my digger cockpit. The first thing I did was change the frequency setting on the radio. Then I did it to all the rest. I didn't want Elena or the Landers to hear anything we might say.

As I finished the last digger, I heard footsteps rush up behind me and something hard smashed into my shoulder blade. I fell to the floor in searing pain, grabbing my arm.

I turned and put my other arm up to defend myself.

Fatima hovered over me, holding a large metal wrench.

"Traitor!" She prepared to slam the wrench down again.

"No!" I yelled. "I'm not a traitor!"

She held the wrench over me. "You lied about the cave-in. You lied about Elena. And now you are sabotaging the diggers so we can't escape."

I shook my head, which sent a whole different kind of pain down my arm. I winced. "No. I was changing the frequency settings on the radios."

She lowered the wrench a bit and cocked her head. "And how is that less suspicious?"

I kept my hand between my face and the wrench but got up onto my knees. "There is a traitor," I said. "She's told the Landers what frequency we've been using."

"They've been listening to us?"

I nodded. "When we've been close enough for them to hear. They've been tracking us. Finn didn't die in a cave-in. We were ambushed."

"You said she."

"What?"

"You said the traitor is a she."

Had I said that?

"You must have suspected me," she said, not lowering the wrench. "I don't blame you. It could make sense." She stared into space, clearly running through the same variables I had considered earlier. Then she lowered the wrench.

"It's not Elena," she said.

"Why not?"

"I can't say."

"Why? Where is she?"

Fatima gave deep sigh. "I don't know for certain."

This was frustrating.

"Maybe the traitor is you, Fatima, and that's how you know Elena is innocent?" I said, looking at the wrench and massaging my shoulder. "Maybe this is your ploy to kill me and make it look like it was me."

She shook her head and threw the wrench against the wall.

"It's not me, Christopher. But if you'd like to set a trap to find out who it really is, I will help. But we've got to be fast."

Chapter Twenty-Six
Trap

Fatima went to fetch the drivers. I told her not to call Therese. I was certain she was innocent, and the fewer diggers involved, the better for our plan. I stayed behind in the garage and leaned against my machine. My heart pounded against my ribs. I needed to calm down.

For our plan to work, I needed to look composed, not suspicious. I focused on the pain in my shoulder. It stung every time I moved my arm too quickly.

I heard footsteps approaching and stood up straight, nodding at everyone as they walked past me and took their positions by their machines.

"There's been a change of plans," I said. "Instead of moving right away, we are going to drive ahead to scout

out a new location. Then we will come back for the supplies."

Jimmi looked at me, confused. "I thought you said there was a danger of a cave-in?"

I shook my head. "No. That was a lie. I needed Darcy and Alek, and maybe even Maria, to buy into the move without panicking. The truth is"—I paused and took a breath—"the truth is that the Landers have been tracking us."

I raised my hands to calm the ensuing racket.

"We don't have time to go over all the details. I hate to tell you this, but Finn was killed in an ambush and I know how it was done."

I'd been hoping someone in the room would look scared or guilty at this point, but they all just looked angry. And so I had to go on to the next, trickier part of the plan.

"How was it done?" Pavel yelled. Did he look scared? Guilty?

I lied again.

"I believe the Landers were tracking us using the warning signals the grinders use. They send out an echolocation blip that gets answered back. The Landers were picking that up and were able to follow us with pinpoint accuracy."

A lump rose in my throat, but I continued.

"The sensors are activated each time a digger is turned on. So the Landers could also use it to find us here. That's why we need to move."

Pavel slammed his fist against his digger. "The grinders must have known that! They've been working with the Landers!"

"I don't think so, but it is a reason to scout a location for the camp without them. A location that we haven't discussed before."

There were some nods.

"Can't they just track us again?" Mandeep asked.

Now we got to the meat of the plan, and the meat of my lie.

"No. I've gone through and disconnected all the sensors in the diggers."

"How do we know where to go?" Pavel asked.

"We'll be traveling through tunnels on the tracks, no disrupter. There are four of us. Each will go in a separate direction, one per tunnel. Then alternate right and left side-tunnels until you find a good location."

They looked at me blankly. "I know it's confusing. I've plotted the sequence into your guidance systems. It's a closed system, so it doesn't send a signal; it just puts a numerical sequence on your screen. When it says third left, you take the third left and so on. It will also guide you back."

"Why not go together?" Jimmi asked.

"This way we can cover way more ground. Each of us will be looking for a location where we can easily set up a camp, sleeping quarters, infirmary . . . all the stuff we have here. One hour out, one hour back. That should give us a new home far enough from here."

There were some grumbles but mostly nods. They'd bought into the plan. Now to set the final piece of the trap.

"Maintain radio silence at all times. Keep your cameras on and be incredibly precise about following the variations on the screen. Is that clear?"

More nods, no grumbles.

"Good, then fire up your diggers, and good luck."

One by one we got in and began to drive away. I followed slowly, dropping back bit by bit until I was sure they couldn't see me. Then I turned on my disrupter and headed into the wall, navigating a path in the rock parallel to the other diggers.

I flicked on my screen. Three red beeps appeared to my left, moving in unison toward the intersection. We reached it in a few seconds, and then they separated.

I waited for a minute and then broke through into

the main tunnel. The red beeps grew brighter without the interference of the rock, and I watched as the diggers began to alternate their turns.

So far, so good. The sensors Fatima had placed in each digger were coming through loud and clear, and none of the drivers were doing anything weird.

Then one of the blips veered off course and dimmed.

One of the diggers had cut into the rock and was heading to the surface.

Chapter Twenty-Seven
Surfacing

I fired up my digger and was off like a shot. Whoever it was had waited just long enough to get clear of the others and then had sprinted for the surface.

Elena was still missing, as far as I knew, but there was no warning signal in her digger, so this couldn't be her. I actually shook with the sense of relief.

The rogue digger was heading up slowly, on an angle away from the camp and toward the surface near the Landers' base. I figured whoever it was, he or she was making sure to be as quiet as possible in case the vibrations could be picked up.

That gave me a short window to act.

I gunned my engine and charted a path a mile or

so ahead of the red beep. I flew in front of the digger's path and cut a hole at a ninety-degree angle across the trajectory. I crisscrossed it again and again, leaving just a thin layer of rock between the different cuts. Then I tore down that wall with my borer. The end result was a giant air pocket, big enough to shut down the disrupter on the traitor's digger, lying directly in its path.

I turned off my engine and waited in the darkness. I didn't want to think about who it could be. I'd know soon enough.

Elena was innocent. Or was she? What if the traitor wasn't acting alone? What if Elena was a partner? No. Definitely not. I was convinced of Fatima's innocence, and she was convinced of Elena's. If only I felt the same connection to Elena that I'd felt before the Blackout.

Then another thought hit me. What if the traitor were working with Fatima and she'd now set me up?

The warning sensor starting blinking again. The digger was getting closer. I reached back behind my seat and grabbed a wrench. Then I flipped open the hatch, stepped outside, flicked off my headlamp, and waited.

I heard a loud buzzing and humming sound. It traveled from my toes to my feet and then my legs as the rock around me vibrated to the disrupter. I took a step backward. I didn't want to be close to the blistering nose cone of the digger, especially not before the sensor turned it off.

The vibrations actually grew calmer as the digger approached the air pocket. Then there was a flash of brilliant blue and a loud pop as the air around the cone exploded. It stung my eyes. *Idiot.* I realized how dumb I was to wait in the pitch black, leaving my eyes unprepared for the sudden brightness.

I heard the digger screech to a halt as the disrupter shut off.

The borer continued to spin, and the driver tried to go on through the other side. He or she hadn't seen me. I only had a short time before the border dug in deeply enough to reignite the disrupter.

My eyes slowly adjusted to the light, and I walked forward, the wrench raised. The glow of the panel illuminated the face of the driver, the traitor.

Jimmi.

He didn't see me yet; he was concentrating on trying to cut through the wall.

I walked back to his engine block. It only took me a few seconds to loosen the two bolts I'd left intact to keep the hood closed. I reached in and yanked the power line, and the digger shut off.

I flicked on my headlamp and walked back to the cockpit.

I smashed the wrench down on the hatch.

Jimmi turned to face me, his eyes wide with panic.

"Get out!" I yelled.

He shook his head.

Coward, I thought.

I got back in my digger and fired up the drill. I aimed it straight at Jimmi and gunned the engine.

He raised his hands in front of his face as my digger flew at him.

At the last second I slammed on my brakes. The end of the bit spun menacingly an inch away from the hull.

Jimmi lowered his hands. His eyes were still wide, and he was shaking.

"Get out!"

He nodded and opened his latch.

I turned off my digger and got out again, still holding the wrench.

"Hands on your head," I said. I didn't know if the Landers had given him any weapons, and I didn't want to find out.

Jimmi put his hands on his head.

"Now, on your knees," I said.

Jimmi got down on his knees.

"I didn't mean for Finn to get killed," he said, sobbing. "They wanted to capture him, capture you. It must have been an accident. It was, wasn't it?"

I didn't say anything. Jimmi wanted to believe the Landers were his friends? I'd let him, for now. I kept the wrench ready in case he tried to escape.

"They said they would let us live if we'd stop attacking them."

"And you believed them?" I said. "When did they tell you this?"

"The first day I was on lookout duty. I turned on my radio. I was bored. I flipped through the frequencies, and I heard them talking." He began to sob. "Christopher . . . I heard the voice of my father."

I lowered the wrench, shocked. "Your father?"

Jimmi nodded. "He was being ordered to talk over their radio, tell the Landers where the different ores were stored. He was alive!"

"So you tried to see him?"

"Not at first. I couldn't believe it was true. But the next time I was on lookout duty, I heard his voice again. He was so weak, but I knew it was him."

"What happened?"

"That day, when I was supposed to take the pictures, I wanted to see him so badly, and then Elena gave me a perfect excuse. I broke through the surface, and they started firing at me."

"And you agreed to betray us to save your life." I was so angry, I raised the wrench again, ready to strike.

He shook his head, more tears flowing. "No. It wasn't like that."

"How else could it be?"

He was now full-out sobbing. "They let me see him. He was in a cell, but he was alive. Then they said if I didn't help them, they'd kill him." He fell to the floor, his chest heaving uncontrollably.

My hand faltered. A few seconds before, I'd been looking at a spy, a traitor, a murderer. Now I saw myself. A kid. A kid whose father had been taken away from him, and then offered back. What would I have done? Would I have cooperated?

"Were there other survivors?" I asked.

"I don't know. I don't think so. My father was in a cell, alone. He was so beat-up, burned. But he recognized me! He told me he loved me. Then they dragged me away and told me they just wanted us to stop attacking until they were done. Then they said they'd let us all live." He began crying again.

"Did you work alone?"

Jimmi nodded. "I gave them our radio frequency. I snuck away to my digger two nights ago and radioed them the plans for the attack, and about the radiation bomb. That was all I told them. I didn't say where the camp was or anything else."

I ran my hand over my face. Now what was I supposed to do? The Landers had obviously lied to him. Maybe it wasn't even his real father. Maybe it was. Maybe he'd wanted to believe so much that he convinced himself they were telling the truth.

Jimmi stared at me. He got back on his knees. "I'm so sorry, Christopher. Are you going to kill me?"

I held the wrench limply at my side. "No."

He stared at me, wiping tears and snot on his sleeve. "Thank you, thank you."

"Go join the Landers. Go be with your father."

I could hear both Elena's and Fatima's voices in my head, as well as Pavel's, yelling at me. *What are you doing? He's going to betray us again! He'll tell them everything! You're giving them a digger!* I ignored the voices.

"I'm going to dismantle your disrupter first," I said. "You can tell them it was damaged."

Jimmi started to stand up, nodding. "Okay, okay. Thank you, Christopher."

"Go stand over there, facing the wall, and put your hands back on your head." I motioned with the wrench. Jimmi nodded and walked over.

I opened up the nose cone quickly and took out

the disrupter's power source and drive mechanism. I doubted the Landers had the technology here on Perses to replicate a digger, but I wasn't going to leave them anything they could use to try.

Jimmi stayed as still as stone, facing the wall. He'd stopped crying, but he hadn't stopped shaking.

"One more minute," I said. He nodded but didn't turn around.

I took a seat in Jimmi's digger and deleted all the data from the locator. I was about to tear out the radio, but then I stopped. Instead I changed the frequency.

Then I got out.

"Jimmi. It's time to go."

He turned around, white as a ghost, shivering as if he had a fever.

He took a step toward me and looked like he was going to shake my hand or maybe even hug me. I refused.

"No," I said. "You didn't see what they did to Finn."

He lowered his head. "It had to be an accident," he said to himself under his breath.

I pointed at the cockpit. "Get in."

Jimmi was breathing quickly. He took his seat and strapped himself in. "I won't tell them anything."

I put my hand up and stopped him from lowering the hatch.

"You're right. What you're going to do is tell me everything you see."

Jimmi started. "What? How?"

I pointed to his radio.

He shook again. "No, they'll hear me, they'll kill me. They'll know!"

"No, they won't. I changed the frequency of the radios. You'll only be talking to me, and you are going to tell me everything you see. Every detail. How many people you see. Where the ship is. Keep talking until you have to get out, then shut off the radio. Do you understand?"

Jimmi nodded.

I let go of the hatch, and Jimmi lowered and locked it. He turned on the digger and waited. I got in my digger and switched on the radio. "Do you hear me?"

"Yes," Jimmi said.

"Good. I'll go ahead and use my disrupter to burn a hole. I'll stop right before the surface, and you will dig the rest of the way."

"Okay."

I stopped my digger just below the ground and then reversed. I watched as Jimmi passed me and headed for the surface. He didn't turn to look, but he started talking.

"I can see the surface. I'm breaking through. There's light."

I turned off my microphone and listened.

"Okay, there's no one around. I'm going to level out.

"I'm not far from the ship. It's a big ship, the one that attacked us. There's just one. I don't see any guards around, but there are a lot of small vehicles, kind of like little tanks. They are carrying containers and are in a circle around the base of the ship.

"Okay, I'm on the level ground now. Turning off my borer. I can see a few larger container vehicles way off to my right. You said be specific, so I'd say two hundred yards directly to my right. They seem to be moving toward the ship, so away from the storage area. They must have built a new road, or are just going off road. There is a lot of dust.

"I don't see any lights on in the other buildings, but it's bright out. A lot of the buildings are badly blasted, like they've been bombed.

"Okay, I'm now about a hundred yards from the ship and am slowing down. It's straight ahead. I'm opening my hatch and waving so I might get quieter."

I could hear Jimmi's clothes rustling as he probably stood up and began waving. Then he yelled to the Landers. "They found out! I need help!"

I heard him sit back down. He began to whisper.

"Christopher. I'm not sure how much time I have before I have to stop talking. The ship is huge. It's right in the middle of the landing pad. It's resting on legs, and the hull is only about a yard or so off the ground. I still don't see anyone walking around . . . Wait, the gangplank is lowering. I'm about fifty yards away, so I'm going to stop. There are about five, no, ten Landers coming down.

"They're carrying something, a bag? Maybe a . . ."

There was a long silence, and I heard Jimmi gasp. When he spoke again, his voice was shaking even more than before.

"It's my father. Oh my g—Christopher, it's my father. They're dragging him down the gangplank. He's not moving, he's . . . no, no, no . . . They lied. Christopher, they lied. . . ."

I could hear Jimmi pounding his fists against the console. It sounded like thunder in my cockpit. I turned my microphone on.

"Jimmi, Jimmi. You've got to get out of there!"

He didn't answer me. Instead he cursed and pounded the console again. I heard his engine roar.

"Aahhhhhhhhhhhhhhhh."

I couldn't see, but I could tell he was driving straight for the Landers.

There were loud cracks and explosions, and then there was nothing.

Chapter Twenty-Eight

Hard Truths

I told everyone the truth about Finn's death and Jimmi's betrayal.

Darcy sobbed and hugged Maria.

Everyone else just went to bed in a kind of shocked silence.

Not everyone.

Elena was still AWOL. Now I was worried. Where was she? Had she gone and done some stupid solo attack? Was she dead?

I didn't know if I could cope with that, especially on top of everything else, and the idea gripped me as I took my turn on guard duty.

I pulled out *Oliver Twist*. Oliver, it turns out, was

really from a wealthy family. His mother had run away in shame, and that was why he'd been born in the poorhouse.

There was a locket that would prove Oliver's heritage, but an evil guy named Monks had thrown it in a river. Charles Dickens put a lot of evil guys into the story. Monks actually turned out to be Oliver's brother, and wanted Oliver dead so he could claim all the family's inheritance.

Luckily for Oliver, Bill Sikes's girlfriend, Nancy, overheard the truth and was going to run off to tell somebody and . . . That was where I'd stopped reading a few days before.

I flipped the pages, knowing some of the numbers were circled, but the code still didn't make any sense, so I decided to lose myself in the final pages.

I flicked on my headlamp and continued reading. Monks was talking about killing Oliver. Fagin and Sikes were having Nancy followed.

I heard footsteps in the tunnel.

Fatima walked up to me and gave me a weak smile.

I realized I'd never told her the code I'd found using the flashlight. Before I could say anything, she spoke.

"I know where Elena is. I think you should go see her."

A horrible sense of foreboding took ahold of me.

"Is she okay?"

"Let's go."

Fatima and I climbed into my digger, and we drove down Tunnel 1. I noticed that each turn we took was based on a simple one-one sequence. Very Elena. Straightforward.

"Stop here," Fatima said. We'd reached the entrance to a newer section of subtunnel. There were no lights.

"She's down there," Fatima said.

I turned off the digger and walked silently into the tunnel.

A soft glow flickered ahead. I leaned a hand against the cool stone of the wall and edged closer. My eyes slowly adjusted to the gloom, and I could see that the light was coming from a flare that had been set into a hole in the wall. A thought flashed in my mind that this might be a trap of some kind, but then I heard the sound of quiet sobs.

Elena was asleep, curled up on a bed of blankets and old clothes on the floor.

Fresh tears were on her face. I knelt down and gently touched her cheek. She was holding a weathered old teddy bear, Hector. I recognized him from when we were kids.

I could feel tears starting to well in my eyes.

Above her makeshift bed Elena had carved out a large hole in the rock. The flare was anchored in a slot next to it, lit like a memory shrine.

There was a picture of her family, taken as they boarded the ship to Perses.

There were books on military strategy, but also a book about a kid detective, and another about a girl who could talk to cats, which had been Elena's favorite picture book.

I took it out gingerly. The cover was singed. I opened it, and a worn scrap of paper fell out from between the pages and landed on the lip of the hole. I caught it before it could fall, and I held it up.

It was a picture that Elena had drawn of her and me. It must have been from second grade. She and I are holding hands. We're staring out from the paper, smiling. *Hapy Valtines dAY* was written on top of a giant red heart. It surrounded us like a crayon halo. My lips trembled as I noticed she'd written *LOVE* overtop of our hands.

I turned it over. There was more scribbled kid's writing.

To: CrisTFer LOv: ELenA

"Christopher?" said Elena at my feet, sleepy.

I quickly tucked the paper into the book and placed it back inside the hole.

"Hi, Elena. Yes, it's me."

"What are you doing here? How did you find me?"

"I was worried about you. Fatima said you were down here."

"Fatima." Elena reached up with her hand. I took it. Her fingers were cold. She was shivering. I held her hand tightly as I got down and sat next to her.

"I didn't know you'd saved so much stuff from your apartment." I nodded back toward the hole.

"Only the most important things," she said.

"We've got to move the camp tomorrow," I said. "I didn't want you to come back and wonder where we'd gone."

"I wasn't sure I was coming back."

I put my arm around her and pulled her toward me.

She looked up at me. "I'm so sorry, Christopher," she said. "I tried to be so strong. But then all of a sudden it was just too much." She bit her lip to stop from crying again. "That little boy we buried."

"Thomas."

"Thomas. It was so horrible. So senseless. I tried to push it all away after that. Just focus on the combat.

That's what I'm supposed to be good at, right?"

I didn't say anything. She'd seemed so emotionless, and I'd misread what she was really feeling. I remembered how red her eyes had looked. How drawn her face had seemed.

"Then I couldn't even do that anymore."

"That's not true. You were a huge part of those raids. We're doing it. We're stopping the Landers."

"Jimmi's recon was my idea, and it was a disaster. I almost got him killed."

I realized with a jolt she didn't know what had happened.

"Elena. It was not your fault. Jimmi was . . . He wasn't what we thought he was."

I explained everything that had happened.

The news hit her hard. "I should have known. He was my partner for those raids."

"He fooled all of us, Elena, all of us."

She cried into my shoulder. "I just can't get all the images out of my head anymore. I feel so pathetic."

"It's okay," I said, holding her. "Elena, you are the strongest person I've ever known. No one should have to see what you've seen. But we're going to get through this. We'll do that together. When I'm weak, you can be strong. When you feel weak, I promise I'll be there for you."

"I know. That's what soldiers do. They look out for each other."

"That's what friends do."

She nodded.

"You're doing an amazing job, Christopher Nichols. If I'd been in charge, we'd all be dead."

"Elena. I said I needed your help. I do. I also need you."

She gave me a weak smile, then tucked her head back onto my shoulder. In no time at all she was asleep.

I sat there for a long time, listening to her breathing, thinking about the picture she'd kept since we were kids, and thinking about what she'd just told me.

Fighting, even just fighting to survive, was taking a toll on all of us. We needed to bring things to a conclusion. A plan was forming in my head.

But I couldn't ask Elena to be part of it.

Chapter Twenty-Nine
Progress

I woke up with a start. I had to flick on my headlight to remember where I was. My back was against the wall. The cold made my shoulder ache. Elena's head was resting on my uninjured shoulder, thank goodness. I tried to move without waking her, but she opened her eyes and smiled weakly at me.

"I was having a dream," she said. "It was nice. We were kicking stones in the school yard."

"Let me guess: we were seeing who could hit the bars on the swing set more times."

"I was winning."

"Big shock there." I ran my finger over her cheek. "We should get back."

"My digger is just down the tunnel," she said. "I didn't want anyone finding it and then finding me. It'll take about ten minutes for me to get there."

"I'll walk you," I said. She took my hand and kept holding it as I helped her stand and we walked back down the tunnel. The warmth between us was returning, and I couldn't help feeling that we had rediscovered our connection, or had at least started to.

Fatima was sitting in the cockpit of my digger, reading *Oliver Twist*. She smiled when she saw us together.

"This is a very funny book," she said. "Nothing like a real orphanage, of course, but very good anyway. And of course it turns out the kid is actually rich. No wonder you like it."

"Did you ever find a map hidden inside?" Elena asked.

"Sort of," I said. "It's not really a map. It's more like a sequence of numbers."

Fatima nodded and held up her special flashlight. "I've been going through them. I've seen them too."

"Any ideas?"

She stared at me for a long time before talking. "I need to ask you a question about your father."

"Like what?" I said. I wasn't sure what she was getting at.

"Did he ever talk about his childhood?"

"Not much. He told me his parents died when he was quite young. I don't even remember having any pictures of them. He said he worked in the mines to support his family."

Fatima nodded. Then she put down the book and rolled up her sleeve. She turned her shoulder to me. Just above her elbow she had two dark *M*s.

"My father had the same tattoo," I said, incredulous.

"It's not a tattoo, Christopher." Fatima rolled down the sleeve. "It's a brand."

"A brand?"

"My dad didn't have a tattoo like that," Elena said, confused.

"That's because, unlike Christopher's father, he had never been a grinder."

I was stunned. "What?"

Fatima nodded. "Your father was a grinder when he was a child. That's where he got the flashlight, and that's where he learned this code."

My head was spinning. "A grinder . . . But it doesn't make sense. He would have mentioned it, wouldn't he?"

"Maybe it was not something he wanted you to know about him, or about the reality of life in the mines."

"Or maybe it was not something he wanted to broadcast," Elena said.

I thought of how the others had reacted to the grinders when we'd first found them, and understood what she meant. I thought back to how angry he'd been when the miner had told him a couple of grinders had been trapped in a cave-in.

I also thought back to the inscription in the book. It said, *When he's ready.* Had my father intended to tell me but had never gotten the time?

But why did my father allow Melming Mining to use grinders if he knew what that was like firsthand?

Fatima interrupted my thoughts. "This code he left in the book is a code grinders use in the mines when we, well, when we want to find something but don't want anyone else to find it."

"Stolen stuff?" I said.

She narrowed her eyes at me. "Or possibly someone who is trying to escape."

"So you can read the code?" Elena asked.

Fatima shook her head. "You need the beginning number, the key, for everything else to make sense. It's like a lock combination. You need the first number, and then you know how many spins to go left or right after that."

"It's not in the book somewhere?" I asked.

Fatima shook her head. "Rack your brains. Did your

father say anything else to you? Anything that might have been the key to the sequence?"

I thought hard, but I came up with nothing. "Why would he make it so difficult?"

"He clearly didn't trust somebody. He wanted the beacon hidden. Even if the map had fallen into the wrong hands, they'd be unable to break the code without knowing the first number."

We sat there for a minute, trying to think of how we could break the code.

I was also thinking other things.

"I understand why this book was so special to my parents now. My dad said he met my mom in the mines. She must have seen him working as a grinder. . . . I wish I could ask them the story now."

"It must have reminded him and your mother of their childhoods. Like I said, there are some very unrealistic parts in this book, but there are also parts that capture the sadness of a lonely life in poverty."

"Wow." I gave a quick ironic laugh. "Maybe this was a perfect birthday present for their baby boy after all."

Fatima looked confused. "Baby?"

I showed her the inscription my father had written in the front.

To Susan
A gift for you and our new baby boy.
Read it to him at bedtime.
When he's ready.
Jim

"But this book isn't that old," she said.

She took the book and opened it up to the information page. I looked at the publication date. This edition was printed after I'd been born. In fact, my dad must have bought it right before we left for Perses.

"Then why would he put that dedication in the book?"

"What day were you born?" Elena asked.

"May twentieth."

"Five twenty," Fatima said. She closed her eyes and starting making lines in the air with her fingers and hands, like she was working out a diagram on a chalkboard.

"You remember all the numbers?" Elena asked.

Fatima didn't open her eyes or stop moving her hands. "It comes naturally. You get used to doing work without textbooks or computers."

Finally she opened her eyes and smiled. "Got it," she said. "The opening sequence is your birthday. The five is the beginning number, and then the sequence continues from there."

Elena and I stared blankly at her.

I shook my head. "Okay, I might need some help figuring that all out."

She looked at me and tsk-tsked. "Rich boy, I thought you were smarter than that. Your dad wouldn't leave you a code you couldn't break."

"I'm not so sure about that. He was trying to tell me something about the map at the very end, right before the elevator doors closed. Maybe it was the key?"

"I will tell you this. The numbers that are circled once indicate left. The numbers that are circled twice indicate right. The numbers that are exed out, alternate left and right, but starting with the opposite of the first direction in the sequence."

I turned to Elena, "Believe it or not, I got that, first time."

"I believe it."

Fatima continued. "Don't worry about specifics yet, like location or distances. Just pick a starting point, and then think of the numbers and how they are telling you which turns to take and see what you get."

I pulled out my notebook and marked an X in the middle of a page. Then I started with five, the first number of my birthday. I used dots so everything would fit on the paper. Following the sequence of numbers, I ended up with a final X in the upper left.

"Now, try it again with a different starting number."

I went back to four and then followed the same sequence after that. I ended up with a second X in the upper right of the paper.

"See? Four was a misdirection. You discard it and start from five," Fatima said.

"One wrong turn and you could find yourself as far away from the right place as possible. It was the same logic I'd used when I came up for a place to set up our first camp!"

Just for kicks I started with nine. I ended up in yet another part of the sheet.

"Wow." I breathed. "That's cool."

Fatima smiled. "Good, so you understand how the sequence works."

"And why it's important to know exactly which number and direction kick things off. I'm not sure I could have figured that all out on my own, especially the left and right variations."

"Perhaps your father knew you'd discover a grinder once you lived in the tunnels long enough. Or he hoped you'd have time to try out different combinations."

"So how do we know what unit we need to measure?" Elena asked. I was glad to see her becoming more engaged again.

"That's twenty. Each unit is twenty yards, twenty feet, twenty tunnels, or twenty miles."

"Or?" I said. "That's a pretty big difference. How do we know which one is right?"

Fatima closed the book and handed it back to me. "You look. I'd suggest trying feet first. It's smaller."

"Thanks, Dad," I muttered to myself.

"And where do we start?" Elena asked.

"There are four tunnels," Fatima said.

We nodded.

"Then I'd suggest starting with number one."

"Okay, then one last thing. What do the numbers in the boxes mean?"

Fatima scrunched up her nose. "I have absolutely no idea."

Chapter Thirty

Modifications

I wasn't even sure it was necessary to move camp, but everyone had already started, stopped, and then started moving again so many times, we needed to see it through. At least it kept everyone occupied.

We'd chosen a spot Pavel had found on his search. There was a break room down Tunnel 1 that still had some canned food and bottled water. There was even a large hall-way a short walk away where we could park the diggers.

And since it was in Tunnel 1, we could spend some of our spare time looking for the beacon.

Maria helped Darcy pick out her new bed. In an odd way they seemed to be helping each other heal. Darcy wasn't talking to me, which hurt. Maria did catch my eye as she helped tuck Friendly into Darcy's bed, and she gave me a weak smile.

Elena, however, seemed way more cheerful as she helped take over the unpacking of all the supplies, barking orders like a drill sergeant.

Talking together had helped, I thought. I knew it was helping me.

That felt kind of awesome.

At some point Alek slipped away. Fatima said she would take Julio and Nazeem and go look for him after we finished work.

We unloaded the food and stacked it in the break room, dug out a new set of bathrooms, and set up the infirmary.

It looked exactly the same as the last camp, with two beds missing.

Time was running out. We needed to find the beacon before the Landers left Perses. And all the evidence pointed to that being very soon, before the end of the Blackout.

Jimmi's father had been the manager of the colony, and he would have been able to tell the Landers everything they needed about how to load the ore, where it was, and how to secure it and process it.

Getting rid of him meant they didn't need him for that anymore.

Getting rid of Jimmi meant almost the same thing.

They didn't need to worry about *us* anymore. They were close to finishing their own Great Mission. I didn't tell anyone else this, although I suspect Fatima knew what was going on. Elena, too, maybe.

We had a map to find the beacon, but it would take time.

Fire the beacon too early, and they'd hear it and destroy it, and us.

Find it too late, and it wouldn't matter. The Landers would already have destroyed the colony, the transmission equipment, and us along with it. The signal might tell Earth there'd been an attack up here, but that wouldn't help us.

So, there were just days left to stop the Landers once and for all. And that meant destroying their ship with as many of them on it as possible.

Jimmi had given me the exact location. He said there were few other buildings left intact, so that meant the Landers most likely slept on the ship.

Of course, the ship had missiles and bombs that could wipe out a digger in one shot. We had nothing.

But I had a plan for all that.

And it was going to begin with another lie.

Everyone continued to set up camp. I snuck away to the garage.

As quietly as I could, I opened the dashboard in my

digger, revealing all the wires and computer chips that controlled the engine and the nose cone. I spotted the wire for the disrupter sensor, and cut it. Then I spliced the wire and pulled a microphone switch out from my pocket. I'd grabbed it from Jimmi's wrecked digger.

I attached the sensor wires to the switch. I flicked it on and off. There was no real, or safe, way to test if this worked, but I just wanted to be sure the flicking didn't loosen the wires.

It didn't. I pulled out some surgical tape and taped the switch to the underside of the steering column. Then I began putting the dashboard back in place.

There was a cough from behind me.

I froze. Someone was in the room. How much had they seen? I hoped it was Darcy or even Pavel. I could lie to them, say that I was just cleaning.

Fatima or Elena would know exactly what I was up to.

I turned around slowly.

Alek was standing behind my digger, staring at the screwdriver in my hand.

"Christopher. I know you're planning something. I've been watching you."

"There are people out there looking for you."

Alek nodded. "I know."

I turned back to my work and finished putting the

dashboard back in place. There was no use hiding the rest of the job from Alek, but I didn't want anyone else seeing my dashboard taken apart and asking questions.

I looked around the garage as I wiped my hands on my coveralls. Something was wrong.

"Alek, where's Maria's digger?"

Alek shuffled his feet and hung his head. "I said before that I wanted to fight. I want to know how to drive one."

"Where is the digger?"

Alek nodded back over his shoulder. "I crashed it in Tunnel Three. It stalled out, and then I went into the wall too fast and smashed the front."

I ran my fingers through my hair. We were starting to get dangerously low on diggers. "I think I can salvage the digger if we can get it back. Does it drive?"

He nodded. "I think so. I was just a little too rattled to try."

"We'll go get it in a few."

"Then we'll fix it, and you can give me some lessons."

I shook my head. "There's no time. We need to do more raids to slow the Landers down some more."

"Christopher. I'm not an idiot. I know I haven't been doing a lot of talking, but I've been doing a lot of thinking. The Landers killed Jimmi. That means they didn't need a spy anymore, which means they are almost done."

This was exactly the conversation I didn't want to have. But Alek was right.

"This isn't going to be a normal raid, is it?" he said.

"No. It's not."

"You're planning something final. I think I know what it is. I know what you did to your digger in the elevator shaft."

I gritted my teeth. "My job is to keep everyone safe, everyone alive. I'm going to do that. If you tell anyone what I'm doing, they'll either try to stop me or they'll try to join in. In either case we'll all get ourselves killed."

Alek stood there, staring at me silently, hardly blinking. Finally he nodded. "I'll promise not to tell anyone, but you have to promise me one thing back."

I knew what was coming, but I asked anyway. "What?"

"You take me with you."

I sighed and didn't answer right away, and then I nodded. He reached out his hand. I shook it.

"The first thing you can do is to keep watch and make sure nobody else comes in here. I just have a couple of more things to do, and then we'll be ready."

"When do we leave?" Alek asked.

"First thing tomorrow."

Alek nodded and then went to stand by the door.

I had no intention of bringing Alek along.

Chapter Thirty-One
Beacon

"So it's agreed," I said, counting the raised hands. "And it's unanimous. Tonight, after dinner, we will send out two search parties to look for the beacon. Fatima will lead one using yards as the distance. Pavel will drive that digger."

Pavel nodded.

"Elena will use miles."

I felt a twinge of sadness and fought to hide it. I hoped it was miles. That would keep Fatima busy on four fruitless searches and Elena far from danger.

Elena was back at her place by my side. She had her arms crossed and a severe look on her face as she said, "If you find the beacon, do not touch it. We cannot set it off until the Blackout is over."

Everyone nodded.

"And Therese has proven she can drive, so I suggest she follow me with Nazeem and Julio in the cockpit," Elena said.

"It'll be tight," Nazeem said.

"Not with your skinny butt," Julio said.

"Or both of your big heads," Therese said. "But if you agree to keep quiet, I can show you how a digger works."

Julio and Nazeem closed their lips tightly.

I made eye contact with Alek. He was keeping quiet and nodding along. Good.

The meeting broke up.

"That went pretty well," Elena said. "Nice job." She gave me a very light tap on the arm.

"Ouch," I said.

She laughed, and it was nice to hear that sound echo in the room.

"I had another great idea," she said. "I'm going to take Darcy along with me. She's been so sad since Finn died."

"That's a great idea. Don't forget to talk to Friendly, too. She gets mad if you ignore him."

She nodded.

I had to fight the urge to say good-bye to Elena, to hold her hand again, to feel her head on my shoulder one last time. But I needed everything to appear normal. Or as normal as anything could be.

"So, I guess we are back to being a pretty good team," I said.

She nodded.

"Can we go for a walk?" she asked.

My radar went off. Had I done something, tipped her off in any way? I did actually promise to give Alek one more quick lesson in digger driving, but I just couldn't leave Elena with the memory of me saying no to her.

"Um, okay. I'd love to." As soon as I even said the word *love*, I felt a lump rise in my throat. I gulped and steadied myself.

She slipped her arm in mine, and we stepped down the tunnel.

"I'm feeling better, Christopher," she said. "I want to thank you for that."

I didn't say anything right away. I was worried I'd start tearing up.

"And you don't suspect me of being a spy anymore, so that's good," she said.

"I know. I'm so sorry. I didn't actually think you were; it's more that I needed to weigh the evidence without letting my emotions get in the way. I couldn't let the safety of the whole camp be compromised because my gir— Because we're friends. If there's anything I can do to make it up . . ."

She smiled again and gave a little laugh as she pushed away from me. "Christopher Nichols, you are still so easy to wind up!"

She took my arm again, and we continued down the tunnel. Elena had certainly recovered her ability to leave me feeling flustered.

"I wonder what will happen after this is all over?" she said.

"I have no idea." I looked at her dark beautiful hair, which was starting to grow back, except for the places where her skin was too badly burned.

"I'm not sure I'm ready to even think about the future yet," she said.

"I think about it sometimes. You need to have hope. Hope that things can get better."

She was silent for a bit as we walked. "We're still not old enough to live on our own," she said, frowning a little.

I was taken aback again. "You mean, together?"

She frowned. "Oh, brother. I mean, without adults. It's like that book you're reading. *Oliver Twisted* or whatever. The kids end up in orphanages or on the streets."

"I'd like to think Melming Mining would take care of us after what we've been through."

"Do you think that includes the grinders?"

I wasn't sure about that. "If you or I have any say about it," I said.

"Adults don't always listen to what kids have to say," she said.

I nodded.

We walked in silence a little longer. "I have a plan," Elena said at last.

Uh-oh.

"I've been thinking about what we can do next."

"Yes?" I said, my voice sounding way too nervous in my own ears.

"We should send up a couple of diggers to the surface."

I gulped but managed to squeak out, "Okay."

"Not to attack, but to dismantle the bombs the Landers set outside the core-scraper."

Whew. "That's interesting."

"I have a pretty good idea where they are. They didn't spend a lot of time trying to conceal them, and I did a walk around before I snuck back into the building."

"You think if we can dismantle those bombs, it doesn't matter if the Landers leave?" I said.

"Exactly. They can't reach us underground. They might be able to drop bombs on the reservoirs and some of the buildings, but they won't totally destroy the infrastructure that way. We can survive and then fire the beacon."

It was actually a pretty good plan, but for one obvious thing—none of us could defuse a bomb.

But I didn't want to argue with Elena.

"I think it's a good plan. We'll call a meeting for tomorrow to map it out with the others, after your team and Fatima's find the beacon."

"You mean after *my* team finds the beacon." She smiled.

"I wasn't aware it was a competition."

She gave me a grin and poked me in the chest. "I think she and I compete for everything."

I gave a nervous laugh. "I guess at the very least it would be nice to be on the surface."

She nodded. "I'll lead the team. I'd like to see the sky again."

We reached the garage. Alek was already waiting there, sitting in the cockpit of his digger and trying to memorize each button and screen. He didn't give away any sign of emotion, any sign he and I were planning to leave.

"I'm going to go prep for the great beacon search. See you later," Elena said. She gave me a quick kiss on the cheek.

Despite my best efforts to stay cool, my lip quivered, and I had to turn away. I coughed, hoping to cover the quaver in my voice.

"See you later," I said, turning back to look at her.

She faced me and gave me a salute. "Fearless Leader," she said.

I saluted back. I watched her walk away. This was the last time I'd be alone with her, ever, and I wanted to hold on to every last image to cherish on the final ride to the surface.

She turned a corner, and I walked into the garage.

Alek looked up at me.

"She hasn't guessed?" he said. He seemed surprised.

"I don't think so. I hope not. Let's go practice."

We spent the next hour driving through tunnels and firing up the disrupter to fly through the walls. Alek was a pretty capable, if not great, driver. Not that it would matter too much. I checked my watch. It was almost dinnertime.

After we ate, Fatima and Elena would start their search. I'd wait a few minutes and then start out on my own.

"Time to head back," I said.

Alek turned the steering wheel, and we cut back through the rock toward camp.

We got out of the digger. "You go grab some food," I said. "I need a few seconds to get myself together."

Alek nodded. After he left, I waited a second, then I opened up the dashboard of his digger and cut the power line.

Dinner was canned beans and chocolate bars again. I didn't want to eat anything, but I forced myself to. Fatima and Elena sat next to me and mostly talked about what the beacon might look like, and how they would keep in contact during the search.

"I think it will be a big computer with lots of colored lights and stuff," Elena said.

"I imagine it will be very small, but shaped like an apple pie," Fatima said.

"With whipped cream icing," Elena said.

"Mmmmmmm," they said, and laughed.

I stared at my beans.

The beacon was the last real connection I had to my parents. They'd helped set it in place. My father had told me to find it. I'd never see it now.

Finally it was time. Dinner ended.

"I walked over to Fatima and hugged her. "Good luck," I said, smiling as cheerfully as I could.

"Thanks, rich boy. Make sure you do all the dishes while we're out doing some real work." She laughed. I rolled my eyes.

Elena was helping Darcy, and Friendly, settle into her cockpit. Darcy had helped save me. I also needed to say good-bye to her.

"See, Darcy," I said, leaning down to hug her. "I told you this was a treasure hunt. I bet you find it first."

She didn't say anything, but looked past me to wave good-bye to Maria. Then she held Friendly's bandaged paw and stared straight ahead.

I stood back up and smiled at Elena. "You stay safe," I said.

"Um, okay. Looking for a beacon? I'll try. You stay safe sitting back here, reading your book."

"Will do." I hugged Elena a little bit longer. I hoped she didn't notice, but I couldn't help myself.

She climbed into her digger, closed her hatch, and then led the mini-caravan of diggers out to the opening of Tunnel 1.

I waited a few minutes before I slipped away to the garage. I'd told Alek we wouldn't be leaving for an hour, so the garage was empty when I got there. I slipped into my digger and fired it up.

I cut through the wall. I didn't head for the Landers right away. I had one important errand to run first.

Chapter Thirty-Two
End Game

I returned to Elena's hideaway.

There was no flare, so Elena hadn't been here since our talk, but I knew she'd be back. I opened the hatch and got out, quickly walking over to the nook.

I turned on my headlamp and reached in for the picture book. I opened it very carefully and stared again at the valentine Elena had preserved for so many years. I ran my finger over the word *love* and cried. I didn't even bother holding it back this time.

I took off my helmet and grabbed the letter from the headband. I carefully tucked it inside the book. I hoped the things I said would help Elena understand what I was about to do.

I put the book in its place and then got back into my digger.

I took a deep breath and closed the hatch. The dashboard lights came on. I realized I was still holding Elena's picture in my hand. Again I stared at the image and the *CrisTFer* she had written on the back.

Then I remembered.

I remembered exactly when Elena had given me the picture. It had been just after we'd started school on Perses. Valentine's Day. She's made it for me and left it on my desk. I'd taken it, thanked her, and then forgotten it when school had ended.

I hadn't thought about it since.

I debated putting the picture back. Then I put it on top of my dashboard.

The quickest path was a straight line from there to the Landers' ship. But I didn't want to be predictable, so I made a few slight turns. That would confuse any sensors the Landers were using to detect someone on the way to attack.

I stared at the picture of Elena and me holding hands, and it calmed me. She was probably getting close to finishing her first search by now. I imagined her and Darcy chatting about what they would do when they got back to Earth. The games they would play and the desserts they would eat.

Halfway through the trip I noticed a red blip on my screen. It was coming up straight behind me.

I was being followed. Someone had grabbed a digger with a warning signal inside. I eased up on the speed and took a sharp right turn. Then I circled back and waited.

The red blip crossed in front of me. I paused a few seconds and then cut through the wall, turning to follow the digger. It stopped just ahead of me. I came up right behind and nudged the back.

The cockpit hatch opened, and Alek stuck his head out.

I popped my latch as well and yelled, "Alek! What the heck are you doing here?"

He was so mad, he was shaking. "You promised me," he said. "You told me you'd take me along."

"I also told you that my job was to save as many of us as I could, and that includes you."

"That's not good enough, Christopher," he said. He began shaking more violently. "You don't understand. You don't understand. I need to fight. I *need* to."

I watched him. His eyes filled with tears. "Why?"

He stared at me, his lips trembling. "Brock. He's dead because of me." He let out a long moan. "When the

Landers started firing, I panicked. I threw him in front of me. They shot him, and I ran. Your father grabbed me and threw me into the elevator. It should have been Brock in that elevator and me on that field."

"Alek, I . . . You can't blame yourself. You panicked. You said that yourself."

He shook his head. "No. We were best friends. He needed me to defend him, and I didn't. I can't bring him back, but I can fight now to save everyone else."

I understood what he meant.

"You have to let me fight," he repeated, shrinking back into his seat.

"I'm sorry I lied."

"I looked for you after Elena and Fatima left. When you weren't there, I knew you'd left me behind. When I tried to start the digger, I realized you were going alone. I fixed the wire pretty quickly and followed."

I sighed. "I am sorry. It's just that this isn't a burden I want to put on anybody else."

"I asked for it," Alek said. "You always think you know what's best for everybody. Sometimes you just need to listen to what other people are telling you."

I nodded. "Okay. No more lies. Here's the plan, but you have to do exactly what I tell you."

Alek nodded, wiping his eyes. "Okay."

"We are going to attack the Landers' ship directly."

Alek nodded.

"We're going to destroy it and everyone inside."

Alek nodded again.

"It's a one-way trip."

Alek nodded one more time, then closed his hatch and fired up his digger.

We arrived underneath the landing pad. The Landers' ship was just a few feet above us, through a thin veil of rock and concrete. It was late, and the Landers were probably settling in for the night. I felt a twinge of remorse for what I had planned. But I knew there would still be plenty of armed guards who'd be shooting to kill as soon as they spotted us breaking through the surface.

Jimmi had tried talking to them. They'd killed him in cold blood. We'd tried hitting their machinery, and they'd responded by killing Finn.

This was the only choice the Landers had left us. Kill or be killed.

I opened my microphone and tapped three times. I looked behind me and saw Alek turn away to my left. I saw a quick flash of blue and knew he'd activated his disrupter and was starting his ascent. There was no turning back.

I closed my eyes and fired my engine. The digger rose higher and higher, faster and faster. The sound of exploding atoms and grinding stone rose to a high-pitched crescendo.

Then, in an instant, we broke through the surface and slammed into the bottom of the ship's hull. The disrupter shredded the metal, and blue sparks illuminated the scene. Alek was only ten feet to my left, his digger also searing a hole in the Landers' ship.

Our disrupters stopped burning, and we fell back down our holes. We went down about twenty feet, then carved a new attack line in the rock. The disrupters reengaged, and we flew back up. Again we burned holes in the hull, and again we fell back inside Perses's crust to recharge.

The hope was that we could hit the same spot each time, gradually burning more and more of the metal away.

We rose a third time. This time, the Landers were waiting. They crouched on the ground on the edge of the ship and fired their guns. They aimed low, thank goodness, trying to avoid hitting their ship. As a result, most of the blasts hit the ground near us, or went wide of their target.

But not all of them.

A pulse struck the hood of my cockpit, shattering the metal supports. A second shot hit the ground but sent large chunks of rock through the air.

Without the hood to protect me, I was hit by a spray of stone.

One ricocheted off the hull of the ship and smashed into my forehead, just under my helmet. A searing pain spread through my head, like it was splitting apart. All I could see was red.

I could taste blood on my tongue.

My disrupter shut down, and my digger fell back down the hole.

I could hear the scrape of the shattered hood struts against the rock walls over my head.

I ducked forward to avoid being scraped myself. The digger landed with a thud, and my engine shut off completely.

My ears were ringing. My head felt like someone had driven a spike into it. I tried to concentrate. I began pushing buttons on the dashboard. The disrupter fired, then turned off. The drill swirled, but why wasn't I moving?

I looked up toward the hull of the ship. There were blue flashes reflecting off the metal. Alek was still blasting the hull. Then I saw something else. White light, from inside the ship. The last hole I'd made had broken through into the interior.

The realization focused my brain. I grasped that the engine had shut off when I'd fallen back. Quickly, I held the ignition button until it roared back to life.

The light above me began to grow smaller. The ship was taking off!

There was only one chance left. It was time to turn off the sensor on my disrupter and make one final ascent straight into the heart of the Landers' ship. The disrupter would stay on, igniting the air inside the ship, turning it into a giant bomb.

I turned on my radio. It didn't matter if the Landers were listening now. "Alek! Alek! I'm going in. Fall back! Get out!"

Alek didn't answer. I looked up. More blue sparks were reflected off the receding bottom of the hull. Alek was continuing to cut into the ship.

"Alek! Get out!"

Again, no answer. Again, more sparks.

I couldn't wait any longer.

I gunned the engine and then reached under the dashboard to turn off the sensor.

My fingers searched and searched but came up empty.

The switch was gone.

The blue light of Alek's disrupter continued to reflect off the hull of the ship.

Alek had taken my switch and used it to disable his own disrupter.

I breached the surface, but the ship had pulled away. I looked to my left, but Alek was gone. I stared at the hole I'd made in the ship. The white light from inside the ship had turned electric blue.

"Alek, no!"

My radio crackled to life. It was Alek.

"Sorry, Christopher," he said, his voice calm and determined. "Please tell everyone I didn't die a coward."

There was a tremendous screaming explosion.

The entire sky was lit up by a giant fireball.

The blast sent my digger careening back down the hole, followed by a cascade of rubble.

Chapter Thirty-Three

Awakening

My head throbbed. I could hear noises around me, but my ears continued to ring.

I struggled to get my arms free to dig myself out. My arms were pinned to my side.

"He's awake," said a voice somewhere in the fog.

Landers! They'd survived. I'd been captured.

Shadowy forms, maybe three or four of them, approached.

I winced, preparing for a blow to my head or a gun-shot between the eyes.

Instead I felt a soft kiss on my cheek. A face took shape.

Elena.

"Sunlight takes a little getting used to after a couple of months in a mine, doesn't it?" she said. She took my hand and squeezed my fingers.

"Elena," I said. Tears filled my eyes. "Is it over?" I croaked.

Elena just nodded.

Fatima came up next to Elena. "We know what Alek did," she said. "We're safe now. The Landers are gone."

All I could do was nod. The effort must have completely drained me, because I apparently fell back into unconsciousness again. The last thing I saw was a hallucination, a vision of my mother and father, alive, standing next to the bed. "We survived," I whispered.

Eventually, days later, I woke up. I was in a hospital room, not in a tunnel lying on a makeshift cot. There was only one place where a room like that existed: the base hospital. It was aboveground to provide easy access to medical vehicles from the colony or the farming district.

The windows must have been shattered in the attack, because the glass was completely gone. A warm muggy breeze was flapping the posters that Mandeep, or a helper, had tacked in place as makeshift curtains. One corner had come loose, and it made little snapping sounds when the breeze gusted. I stared at it.

WE ARE WHAT MAKES MELMING MINING GREAT. WE ALL WORK TOGETHER.

I could hear the sounds of kids playing soccer, or something, outside. Darcy's laugh carried into the room, and I choked up.

"So, Fearless Leader, are you with us for a while this time?"

Elena's voice, a wonderful sound.

I turned to face her and smiled. "I hope so," I said, wincing at my stiff muscles.

She was sitting on a chair next to me. She had bags under her eyes and looked exhausted but beautiful. Her hair had grown even longer. She reached her hand out to me, and I reached my left hand to touch her. I stopped. I was missing two fingers, my middle finger and ring finger on my left hand.

Elena's lips quivered. "We thought you were dead. When we found you, your body was so bloody and twisted. We needed to cut the digger apart before the hole caved in around you . . . more than it already had. It wasn't a very precise operation under the circumstances."

"It's a pretty small price to pay," I said. "And, hey, I can make the *I rock* symbol with my hand way easier now!" I threw my hand into the air and stuck out my tongue.

Elena laughed so hard, I thought I'd cry.

"How did you find me?" I asked after we'd calmed down.

"As soon as I found the beacon, I dropped Darcy back at camp."

"The beacon!" I said. "Did you fire it off? What does it look like?"

"Whoa, one thing at a time. I'll get to the beacon in a second. But back to your original question. It took me and Fatima all of two seconds to figure out that you and Alek had both left with diggers."

"So?"

Elena frowned at me. "Fatima realized at least one of you had to be in a digger with a warning signal inside."

"You were able to follow Alek."

"Not right away. But when we couldn't pick up the signal closer to the camp, we knew you were heading farther away. You weren't looking for the beacon, so where could you be heading?" She stared at me, her lips pursed but trembling.

I looked away. "I didn't want to put anyone else in danger, so I needed to keep the plan a secret. Alek only found out by accident."

Elena shook her head and pointed her finger at me. "Don't you ever do that again. I'm not kidding. From now on, you do not shut me out."

"I hope I never have to come up with a plan like that again."

"I'm not talking about strategy, Christopher!"

I was confused.

"I got your letter," Elena said.

My cheeks turned red. I'd said a lot of things, personal things, in that letter. Stuff I just couldn't tell Elena face-to-face.

She tossed the letter onto the end of the bed. "I didn't read it, Christopher. I'd like to think I didn't have to, to know what you'd say."

I took the folded paper in my hand and turned it over again and again. Was Elena asking me to say those things now? Why was I still so flustered and confused? My head started to hurt again. Elena was clearly waiting for me to say something. But what?

The door slammed, and Pavel ran into the room.

"Guys, there's a signal coming from Earth!" Then he ducked back into the hallway. The door swung on its hinges.

I turned to Elena, but the moment had passed. She was standing, smoothing her shirtfront. She didn't look at me.

"We did find the beacon. It wasn't a pie with whipped cream. Darcy was very disappointed."

"Which sequence was right? Yards or miles?"

"It's always about the codes with you, isn't it? Not surprisingly, given your love of threes, Tunnel Three was the right starting point," she added, shaking her head. "And it was definitely miles. If it had been yards, we'd have found you and Alek before the attack."

"So what was it like?"

"It was more like a giant series of connected disks very close to the surface. The numbers in the squares turned out to be the code that activated the emergency signal. We triggered it two days ago, after we were certain all the Landers had died in the explosion. The signal has been going out ever since. Of course, the Blackout only ended today."

Today? I'd been out cold for nearly two weeks!

I struggled to get up. Elena put a hand on my shoulder. "I'll get a wheelchair. We should all hear this message together," she said.

She left. I went to put the letter on my bedside table. Elena's picture was there, burned a bit around the edges and ripped and taped back together.

I tossed my letter to the side. I resolved to tell Elena what was in the letter as soon as she came back.

The door swung open again.

"Elena, I do . . ."

It wasn't Elena; it was Mandeep. Elena followed behind her, pushing a wheelchair.

I shut my mouth and closed my eyes. *Idiot*, I thought, again.

"This is not a good idea," Mandeep said. "He shouldn't move too much."

Elena rolled her eyes.

"I'm in charge here, and I demand to be let go," I said. "And I'm not taking a vote."

Mandeep looked angry, but she and Elena eased me out of the bed and onto the wheelchair.

It hurt—a lot. Elena carefully tucked some blankets around my legs. I tried to grab her hand, to try to send her some kind of signal. But she quickly walked around behind the chair and began to push me down the hallway.

So many questions were left unanswered. Who were the Landers? Who were they working for? Where had they hidden before the Blackout?

Maybe whoever was answering our distress call could help.

The hallway ended outside a small office.

Pavel was sitting on a chair in front of a radio receiver, squeezing his headphones tightly over his ears.

He looked up when he saw me come in, and

dropped the headphones around his neck. "The Landers destroyed all the other stuff, so I grabbed this one from a digger. It's tuned into the same frequency as the beacon."

"Nice work," I said.

He put the headphones back on and turned to the radio. "It's started up again."

Every few seconds or so he'd scribble something down on a sheet of paper. Then he took off the headphones. "I've had to listen to it a few times to be sure, but I think I got it all," he said.

He handed me the paper.

> They are coming to get you.
> They are coming to get you.
> They are coming to get you.
> They are coming to get you.

I looked at Pavel, who smiled. "It's been repeating that same message for about five minutes now."

"Yes! Rescue!" I said. Elena hugged me.

We all began dancing around the room. Fatima and Mandeep gave each other a high five.

Pavel twirled in his chair.

Then he cocked his head.

"Wait, there's something else coming through."

He clasped the earphones back over his ears and began decoding the message. He closed his eyes, concentrating, then grabbed his pencil and began writing.

He handed me the paper, a stunned expression on his face.

I read it with a growing sense of alarm.

They are coming to get you.
They are coming to get you.
Hide.
Hide.
Hide.

ACKNOWLEDGMENTS

It takes so many people to make a book. (In fact, go see the acknowledgments for my book *Neil Flambé and the Bard's Banquet* for a good sense of how a book is put together).

For this particular book . . .

Thanks go to Jon Anderson and Justin Chanda from Simon & Schuster, who let me pitch the idea to them over dinner at Remi in Manhattan. Thanks to my agent Michael Levine for helping get us together, and for so much more. (And thanks to the chefs at Remi for an amazing Funghi e Pasta di Tartufo Nero!)

Ruta Rimas took over the book and does what great editors do, kick my butt at every stage to make the book better. She is a great editor for sure, and I am extremely lucky she was there to help me.

Thanks as well to Dominic Harmon who designed the cover and Sonia Chaghatzbanian who designed the whole package.

And thanks to copyeditor Kaitlin Severini, who picked over the book with a fine-toothed pencil!

The seeds of MiNRs go way back in my life.

My brother Mike was obsessed with space. We'd all spend sweltering summers roaming the Smithsonian Air and Space Museum in Washington, DC, but Mike was the kid who had to have the model of the Enterprise on top of a 747.

Mike died before the first shuttle launch, but that love of space has stayed with the rest of us in different ways.

In fact, there are certain space things you need to know about me (and my family is sick of hearing me repeat).

2001: A Space Odyssey is my favorite movie by far.

I saw *Star Wars* 11 times in the summer of 1977. I've probably seen it a hundred times since, although *The Empire Strikes Back* is actually the best of the trilogy.

The Ewoks and the rereleased versions make me sad.

Greedo did not shoot first.

Jar-Jar Binks is an abomination.

And *Star Trek* . . . what can I say? The original TV series is quoted daily in my house. *Wrath of Khan* was the first movie we saw with my mum after Mike died, and it's still one of the best films of all time. Heck, I even like the movie with the whales.

Later on it was *Firefly*, recommended by my brother Tim. Such a great show.

The Iron Giant is my favorite animated movie. So thanks to Brad Bird for that.

National Geographic gets special thanks from me. They made a map of the Universe that I taped to the ceiling above my bed. It showed both how insignificant we humans are, and how amazing it is that we exist. Life is an improbability, but something to be treasured and protected.

And I'd also implore anyone reading this book to take a truly hard look at the practices of mining companies around the world.

Exploiting children does happen in real life.

We need the materials, yes. But the people who mine the precious minerals deserve dignity and a part of the profits.

And that's it for now. Look for more spaced-out thanks in MiNRs #2.